The Christmas Room

Also By David Ralph Williams

GHOST STORIES
Olde Tudor
The Creaking Death
By a lantern's light
Dead Men's Eyes
Sacred – Ghostly Tales

ANTHOLOGIES
Icy creeps, gothic tales of terror
The Paranatural Detective Agency

The Christmas Room

By David Ralph Williams

First issued in 2021 by LOXDALE
PUBLISHING HOUSE

Original cover design by David Ralph Williams.

All other graphics used internally
were produced by the author.

A special thank you must go to Cathy
Start for her hard work helping to get
this book ready for Christmas.

I would like to thank you the reader for
choosing this little book amongst the
multitudes of other titles waiting to be
discovered. I am forever thankful.

The Christmas Room

For my parents Hilda and Ralph.
Thank you always for building the bridge
across the river of time and allowing me
to relive all those yesterdays and become
a child again every Christmas.

How soon hath Time, the subtle thief of youth,
Stol'n on his wing my three-and-twentieth year!
My hasting days fly on with full career,
But my late spring no bud or blossom shew'th.

Sonnet 7: How soon hath Time,
the subtle thief of youth
BY JOHN MILTON

Chapter I
A house of ice.

It was the night before my return to England and I had the same dream last night, the same one I have had since I was a little girl, constant and unchanged. I suppose that it could be called a nightmare, only it is now so familiar to me that I feel no dread or fear from it, only curiosity and afterwards when waking, a terrible feeling of mourning and of sorrow as though I am suffering the greatest loss a person can possibly feel. In my dream the house stands as it has always stood, desolate and prominent against the stark robe of winter. Its great doors open, and yawning are held agape by the drifting snow; granting winter's touch to enter and roam freely and to cover all of the once fine furnishings within with its pristine icy whiteness.

In the dream as ever, I enter the house where the coldness within its walls falls upon me like a blanket made from the snow itself, and the wind blows a steady lamenting wail. I can feel the winter's breath upon my skin and the clothes

I wear feel much thinner than they are within that frosty space. I walk across the grand hall, its festive garlands of holly and ivy now hanging in tatters, and I carefully step over and around the corpses that are half buried under the drifting snow. Those old yet now familiar faces, with their mouths wide open and filled with ice and their eyes staring and chalky, spotted and blood flecked with tears frozen upon the cheek, and all preserved as they had fallen within the frigid tide. The huddles of chairs and tables around the margins have the appearance of being wrapped in fleece, yet under such an icy glaze they are bereft of warmth or softness. The twin staircase sparkles as though it has been fashioned from iced cake and sprinkled with sugar, and icicles plunge from the balustrade as I scale the crystalline steps to the balcony above.

Each bedchamber I visit is sealed from the stroke of winter, yet the air within is as cold as the day outside. The beds themselves with curtains parted, reveal the lifeless occupants; the frozen statues with tormented faces and mouths ajar and hands reaching into the shadows. A wintery draught then forces its way into the room, and I am certain that something else has entered with the wind. I hear the voice again as I have heard it all these years, almost a whisper, a solitary voice, a pleading voice. The sound of a child full of sorrow, of loneliness. A nameless child. Within the house the voice has a sound to it, a feeling that it

9

belongs to a name that shouldn't be spoken. In my dream I search as I always do, yet no child can I ever find.

Chapter II
Arrival at Star Lake Hall

C laude is the best thing in my world, he is the king of my heart, and our union is clearly a blessing for us both. Each day I feel so lucky to have him as my own. Every woman the world over dreams of the perfect husband; a love who is handsome, kind, most patient, forgiving, compassionate, and industrious. All these women may dream away for none can truly know that the perfect husband's heart has already been won. Claude's love has provided the wings my soul yearned for, and I feel that we have both achieved the highest level of love possible.

My dearest parents were the engineers of our initial acquaintance when they organised a social dance at Holly Lane House, my home in Norfolk. He was presented to me by a mutual friend and after we danced, he offered me his card with a desire to escort me for a walk to church the following Sunday and I gladly accepted. Over time I kept a diary of our courtship and inside I stored all the romantic letters he wrote to me. Eventually we had both exchanged tokens of affection: such trifles as trinkets, miniature portraits, and locks of hair. Never wanting to appear flirtatious I carefully used everything in my power to convey the message of my affection for him. I opened the way for his approaches as best as I could towards a gentleman whose heart I honourably desired to obtain.

Over time I kept a diary of our courtship and inside I stored all the romantic letters he wrote to me. Eventually we had both exchanged tokens of affection, such trifles as trinkets, miniature portraits, and locks of hair.

His proposal was made in person, unlike so many of my friends and cousins who had received theirs by way of a letter. I was so very relieved because I began to doubt my good fortune as I listened with fear to so many jealous rivals who attempted to forewarn me that Claude was simply trifling with my affections. I began to wonder if I had indeed so badly misconstrued his advances but as he stood before me in the meadow that morning, with the sunlight painting his azure eyes and softening his dark curls with honeyed tones, he spoke with a tremble in his voice and he told me afterwards that he suffered a tingling through every limb as he asked the question I had longed to hear.

"Dearest Arabella, will you tell me what I most wish to know? The one word that would make me the happiest man alive in the world today!" said he.

"If I can, I will," said I, and could hardly contain my excitement at the prospect of hearing the remainder of his discourse.

"Then tell me of the happy day when you will gladly become my wife!" he finished, and I answered telling him that no sooner day could arrive. My soul blooms as I recall our first kiss. A breeze stirred the long grass and scattered the wishes from hundreds of dandelion-clocks, and they were caught up in our hair and upon our clothes and we ran like dizzy children to bring the news to my parents, who of course both knew of Claude's intentions. My father produced his best wine from the cellar, and we all celebrated and basked in the happiness that the afternoon had brought.

We married in June, it was Claude's wish as 'Juno' was the Roman goddess of marriage, and it is claimed should bring prosperity and happiness to all who marry in her month. I wore a white dress with a lush skirt on the crinoline sewn from lace and silk, and a veil of lace and clear cotton attached to a flower wreath of orange blossoms. I recall as we left the church the sound of the hymns; the joining of unique voices to form the sweet songs and the graceful notes that soared like angels to echo beneath the rafters. After the breakfast at my family home, we left in a carriage drawn by white horses as the merry crowd, made up of family and friends, showered us again with rice and satin shoes hoping that such a nuptial bombardment would induce luck and seal our good fortunes as we embarked on our honeymoon.

We travelled to Venice by steam ship and docked at one of the main ports, then took a smaller ship to the 'Piazaetta' and marvelled at the columns of 'San Marco'. Claude chose Venice because the city's name is derived from the Indo-European root word *wen* meaning 'love'. It is an elegant city, with pleasing architecture. We sailed in a gondola along the 'Grand Canal' and admired the 'Rialto Bridge', and all the splendid palazzos. Our own hotel was divine, and we sojourned for most of the month before finally returning home, sad to be leaving such a glorious city but happy at the prospect of arriving at what was to be my new home and life with my husband, whom I loved with all my heart.

***

I had only visited Star Lake Hall once; the night my family and I were invited to dinner following the announcement of our engagement. The country was in the depths of winter, and it was the darkest and tempestuous of nights. The rain fell heavily, and the wind blew strong as though it was blowing its last breath. We all dashed from the carriage to enter the house quickly to prevent the weather from spoiling our appearance for what would be my first meeting with my future relations. Once inside we were attended to with the most anxious courtesies and were made to feel very welcome. The celebration that night was happy and cheerful and neither I nor my parents had cause for any feelings of apprehension about the house. It was a warm and inviting place filled with a cheerful atmosphere, and I confess I felt very much at home. My only concern was the rather chilly reception I received from Claude's only sibling and sister Viola, who, for some indeterminate reason seemed to take a disliking to me, and try as I could, my approaches towards her made in the most affable manner always seemed to be rebuffed.

15

I can only express my utmost shock and subsequent feeling of foreboding, as I sat next to Claude in the carriage, my hand in his as the horses drew us along the track. We approached the house that sat bathed in the brightness of a July morning. I could now finally see Star Lake Hall in all its glory and recognised it to be the house from my dream. During those moments as the house loomed nearer, I felt cocooned in what I can only describe as a surreal moment, an uncanny feeling as though I had sat beneath the sun feeling its warmth as it shone brightly in a night sky or watched delicate flakes of snow rising upwards instead of falling, it was almost a feeling of time flowing backwards. I saw the profile of a figure in an upper casement, the room behind was lit but its light was washed away by the glare of the sun. I had the impression that it was a man, and I thought that it may have been Claude's father watching our approach with anticipation, or perhaps a manservant. Whoever it was, and for some inexplicable reason, I felt a tingle of menace as I watched the hazy figure being erased by the reflection of clouds upon the glass.

I was only half aware of Claude's chatter as he suddenly became enlivened when the carriage finally stopped in front of the grand entrance. His voice was being muted by my own thoughts as I tried to make sense of this new unexpected revelation: how it was this house where since a child, I had experienced such a sombre tragedy that so often re-enacted itself as I slept. It was the entrance of the house that starkly rekindled the echoes of my dream; the heavy door flanked by stone pillars daubed with blots of lichen. As the door was opened, I could see the visions of the icy rooms beyond, and the broken dead things with their faces in tatters covered with a powder of snow.

An elderly man stood at the doorway wearing the livery of a butler. It was Baxter for I recognised him from my previous visit, as he had been present throughout dinner. He was flanked by two younger men, one shorter than the other but stouter and sturdier of frame. My carriage door was opened by Baxter, and he took my hand and helped me down the step to the gravel below. Claude was quickly by my side.

"Welcome home sir," said Baxter to Claude, who then turned and presented me with a brief bow. "My Lady," he added.

The two younger men began to unpack our luggage from the carriage as Claude took my hand and we followed Baxter into the house.

I stood in the grand entrance hall in front of the extravagant twin staircases, the dark woods of the balustrading and rich carpeted stairs now a far cry from the frozen and frosty ascent I had endured countless times in my dreams. Instead of the immaculate icy whiteness there was intricate ceiling plasterwork, exquisitely carved wooden mouldings, polished panelling and flooring, and beautifully decorated windows of colourful glass. This could hardly be the same place as the house in my dreams and I kept telling myself this yet, I knew in my core that it was. How I failed to recognise the house during my initial visit I must simply put down to my worries and tensions of meeting with my future in-laws because that evening I was consumed with a desire to make such a good impression upon Claude's family. As I became aware of the approach of Claude's mother and sister, I regained control of myself and for now, I tried to forget all presentiments regarding Star Lake Hall.

We were greeted by Lady Darlington and Viola, and I was received with the most cordial welcome, from my mother-in-law at least. Viola although pleased to see Claude, only barely regarded me and usually from under a scowl. It was a situation that needed a resolution but for now I was only eager to settle in at my new home and to find answers to the puzzles that my dreams evoked. Lady Darlington took my hand as she spoke about the preparations for our return to Star Lake Hall.

"We were not expecting you until at least tomorrow afternoon. We have put you in the East wing; I have had the room redecorated, I do hope you find it pleasing," she said, as she presented me with the warmest of smiles and her gentle blue eyes, the same shade as Claude's, regarded me with a softness I had only previously encountered when looking at the face of my own mother.

"I am sure it will be delightful, thank you Lady Darlington but you shouldn't have gone to so much trouble," I replied.

She then looked at me with some amusement and the corners of her eyes crinkled as she spoke again.

"Oh goodness, there must be none of that 'Lady Darlington', please Arabella. You must call me *Mother*, or at least Dorothea!" she said.

I apologised and she released my hand and warmly embraced Claude. I appreciated her sentiments, but I knew there was no one else I could ever call Mother.

"Is Lord Darlington not at home?" I asked, still thinking of the figure at the window that I had observed watching our approach to the house.

"Oh, my husband is out riding he like me was not expecting your return today. He will be very glad to see you both, he has spoken of nothing else since the wedding!"

I now wondered who could have been standing at the window. As I thought of it, I began to feel a little unsteady as light-headedness swept over me. The floor began to undulate beneath my feet as though I was back upon the sea, and I reached out and gripped Claude's arm to steady myself as

I thought I might faint. Try as I could to hide my dizzy spell, Dorothea had observed my sudden falter and reacted with sincere concern.

"My dear Arabella, are you unwell?"

Suddenly I was aware of all eyes upon me, and Viola's in particular seemed to draw some delight from my condition. I regained my composure as the feelings dissolved and offered an explanation as best as I could muster as I wasn't usually disposed to such a weakness.

"I must apologise, it was the voyage home, the sea was somewhat rough, and I was prone to bouts of seasickness, especially at night."

I wasn't sure if this was the reason for my sudden feelings of giddiness, but I could see my answer was accepted for what it was, and Claude placed an arm around my middle before Dorothea spoke again.

"You must rest a while. Please take an hour or so to recover fully from your journey. I have had the room aired and your clothes and other belongings should have been taken up by now."

I watched as she operated a bell pull and seconds later Baxter appeared.

"You rang My Lady?" Baxter uttered.

"Mr Baxter would you please show Arabella to her bedchamber."

Baxter nodded and motioned for me to follow him. I apologised for my apparent need for rest but in truth I *was* tired, and a short interval alone would fortify me, I was sure of that. I told Claude that I would be fine and followed Baxter as he led me to the grand staircases, and as I climbed them, I recalled the way they had appeared in my dream, a frozen, glittering, brilliant flight of steps.

Our bedchamber was delightful, and I could see how much effort Dorothea had dedicated in order to make the room so comfortable and elegant, with many little touches as only a woman knows how to do. I checked the large mahogany wardrobe and adjoining chests of drawers and was satisfied to find my clothes and other personal effects neatly stowed away or placed upon the furniture about the room. The bed was a four-poster and very grand, with the rich curtains drawn and held by ties to expose the frilled top sheets and matching frilled and embroidered pillows. It looked very enticing and the thought of spending an hour or so upon it was appealing. There was a water bottle with a crystal glass on top of a low chiffonier, and I poured myself a drink and took it over to the single casement.

As I sipped at the cool water, I looked out across the grounds below. The lawns were like vast emerald velvetine cloths rolled outwards from the house and were fringed with flower borders in spectacular colour that produced a rainbow rising from the earth. The trees swayed in the warming breeze and were dressed in their best, lush, dark colours with leaves large and open towards the sun's golden rays, and the sun itself, a burnished orb in a blazing blue sky. The window was slightly ajar and the sweet aroma of summer flowers from a climbing rose had filled the room together with the songs of birds, those tiny friends of quill who adorn the sky releasing their soprano song; sweet notes unwritten as a score and played without instrument and never stunted by the unkindness of a cage.

I sat for a moment at a console table and looked at my countenance within the pier glass. Sleep weary eyes looked back at me, all puffy, and beginning to show the early bloom of shadow. I now felt incredibly sleepy, and I lay down upon the bed and closed my eyes waiting for sleep's dream to find me in its wily way.

I awoke to a rattling sound and sat up upon the bed and glanced at a small travelling clock on the table next to me. It was almost mid-afternoon; I had slept for nearly three full hours. I felt hot, the sun had wandered about the room to finally rest upon the bed, and I was perspiring. The jingling resumed and I looked to the door and listened to the noise; it came as though a presence loitered behind it and fumbled with the handle. I called Claude's name hoping it was he, perhaps the handle had seized but I received no reply.

I got up and straightened my clothing that had become somewhat crumpled and approached the door. It opened easily and the passage beyond was empty. I toyed with the handle to see if it was possible to replicate the sound but I could not.

It was so very quiet, so peaceful as I stood outside my bedchamber. A clock chimed from an indefinite place within the house, and I closed the door intending to find Claude and the rest of the family, but I was stopped in mid stride when I felt a tugging of my skirt and thought I had managed to snag it by some means on something in the passage. When I turned to look the only thing at my immediate location was a door, and I am not exactly sure why but I was drawn to it, almost compelled to enter the room beyond.

The door was not locked, and the room was shuttered and void. It had a musty smell that only comes from such places where the windows have not been opened for some considerable time. The wallpaper was all roses and small birds, and articles of furniture were covered by sheets, but I could see that its purpose was as a nursery. I then realised why Claude and I had been placed at the east wing; as newlyweds it made perfect sense for our bedchamber to be so close to the nursery. My heart sang a lullaby at the prospect of Claude and I starting our own little family and this nursery itself, for all its abandonment, was nevertheless endearing. I wandered around passing between shafts of light made visible by the dust motes in the air as the sunlight forced its way through slats in the shutters.

There was an assortment of dear china dolls upon the chimney piece, and a timeworn rocking horse near the window and I pictured Claude riding it as he must have done during his infancy and such imaginings placed a smile upon my face. There was a small-framed bed and a short bookcase crammed with story books with cracked spines from being read so often. I picked up one of the books and the pages were loose and slipped from the bindings and as I bent to retrieve them from the floor, I thought I heard a whisper; a low sibilant voice speaking, soft and quiet, only just discernible. I stopped to listen again holding my breath because the sound had been so slight, and the noise from my heartbeat and the flow of air in my ears grew louder and louder still.

The shock of a hand upon mine caused me to jolt. I turned and saw Claude and his smile slipped when he saw my own look of fear.

"Dearest Bella, whatever is wrong?" he asked. "I came to wake you but you were not in the room; we are about to have tea!"

His brow was furrowed, and he looked so concerned I immediately erased the fright from my face so as not to worry him further.

"You startled me so, it is very quiet in this part of the house."

My heartbeats had subsided, and I reassured Claude that I was fine, and I spoke of how agreeable our bedchamber was. He turned me to face him.

"Are you certain there is nothing wrong?"

I nodded but his eyes said he did not believe me.

"I used to play here in the nursery, and sometimes, when I was alone …"

He stopped talking as his mind remembered things, perhaps that he had not thought about for such a very long time. His eyes stopped seeing mine, they were seeing something else, a time and a place so very far away from the here and now. Claude's reverie passed quickly, and he continued. "As a boy the stillness of this room and the house scared me, almost as though it was whispering secrets to me. Oh, it is nothing Bella, a house as old as this has many sounds but to a small boy sometimes they can be frightening. I just don't want you to feel afraid here, it is your home now, and I hope you grow to love it as much as I."

"Oh Claude, you must think me very foolish indeed!" I said, and then he took both of my hands and kissed them tenderly.

"I would rather spend foolish times with you Bella, than consign myself to the mundane and the common place with any other woman," and again as usual, his words lifted my soul and soon we were both descending the grand staircase arm in arm.

We took tea and a late lunch in the garden

and the whole family was present. Claude's father, Lord Darlington greeted me warmly and asked about our time in Venice and listened with such a keen interest whilst Claude and I described the beauty of all the magnificent palazzos. I mentioned how I had attempted to capture them with my watercolours, and this generated an interest with Dorothea who it transpired, was something of a keen amateur painter herself.

I was hungry as we had skipped breakfast that morning in order to catch the coach to Star Lake Hall and the table in the garden was laid with an enormous amount of the most delightful food. There was a joint of cold roast beef and sandwiches made from thick-cut bread with salted meat and lettuce, as well as delicious jam puffs and fruit cake. There was it seemed so much food for just the five of us, I wondered if all meals at the Hall were so excessive. To drink there was sherry, lemonade, and plenty of tea and it was a most agreeable time. I sat and listened to the family, my new family, as they made merry and spoke light of such blessedly simple matters, and they made me feel so much a part of them. Even Viola was behaving mannerly, and I thought of my own parents, and I missed them deeply and wished they could be here with us in the garden enjoying this lovely summery day.

The uneaten food was cleared away in a timely fashion by the servants but we stayed in the garden well into the afternoon. It was a glorious day, not too hot as it had been in Venice. The garden was bathed in a playful light, and I watched the darting squirrels as they leapt from bough to bough and the birds were in voice and the chorus of the garden rang in my ears. Lord Darlington it emerged, had a keen interest in the garden and in botany itself. He asked me if I found the gardens at Star Lake Hall agreeable and he was overjoyed when I told him how lovely they were and how I would like to paint them and then he rose from his seat.

"Arabella permit me to give you a tour of some more of the gardens," he said, and he offered me his arm to take, and I walked with him to a tranquil walled garden filled with delightful flowers in full bloom. Leading out of this garden was a central avenue of trees pruned in such a way as to create an arched wooded tunnel. We both walked through the tunnel and I listened as he pointed out a rich variety of shrubs and other vegetal specimens, all of which he spoke about in the manner of a naturalist.

"Grass itself doesn't make a garden Arabella; it restrains the natural flora. Oh, show me a woodland or a forest and I will show you a place where Mother Nature thrives!"

We emerged into a clearing, and I was somewhat surprised to see that far to my left was an area of the grounds that appeared to be in disarray, an untamed tangle in an otherwise orderly plot. It was a place of stalwart brambles that strangled what I imagined may have once been an attractive summerhouse. The old structure was circled by dead trees with broken boughs stabbing cruelly at the sky. I stopped to look over at it but before I could ask Lord Darlington why it had been so neglected, he advised that I should not go near the place.

"The whole area is unsafe, the trees are brittle and often break in the wind, and there are roots that hook the feet. Viola had an accident there as a child."

I was about to ask him why he had not simply cleared the patch but he quickly steered me away towards a towering glass house nestled among some shapely clipped hedging.

"If you would indulge me, it would please me greatly to show you a passion of mine, my collection of *Nepenthes* plants," he said, and we entered the glasshouse.

At once I felt hot and clammy and the air seemed thin and stifling. The space was filled with plants of all shapes and varieties.

I was guided over to a crop of unusual plants, and I could smell them before I came close. It was more of an odour than a fragrance; it was a blend of sweet and fetid.

"These are my delight Arabella, and I do believe they are rarely found on these shores."

I watched as he looked over the plants with an expression of pride on his face.

"What are they?" I asked.

"They are quite rare and beautiful plants my dear, and quite carnivorous."

"Surely not!" I replied in disbelief, as I had never heard of such an idea that a plant could possibly be flesh eating.

"Indeed they are," he said smiling. "I collected some specimens during an expedition to the islands of Java and Sumatra when I was a younger man. I was quite taken with them and have managed to propagate them here at Star Lake Hall."

He pointed out the different varieties but to my untrained eye they all looked alike, with climbing stems and sword shaped leaves and vines that ran into locks and curls and formed jug-like structures, complete with adjoining lid that resembled the Bavarian ale mugs that had become the fashion. Underneath the plump, fleshy lids, there seemed almost to be a pair of crimson lips.

"You said they were carnivorous but what do they eat?" I asked.

"Mostly insects but the larger specimens can capture small rats or mice."

"How can a plant eat a mouse? Do they have teeth?" The very idea of a plant with teeth I found to be rather ghastly.

Lord Darlington laughed. "Oh no my dear, not teeth, not in the sense that you or I have."

He called me closer to examine one of the jug-like structures and he held open the waxy cap and I peered inside and saw a juice that filled the fruit-like pitcher and there were a myriad of flies and moths ensnared within.

"The insects, *or* mice are lured into the cup-like mouth; the insides of the cup are slippery, and they are unable to climb back out. At this point they drown or die of exhaustion, and then they are slowly dissolved in the liquor within, a kind of chemical teeth. Oh, I am not a scientist, and I don't really understand; I grow them for their beauty and the interest."

"I am not sure I could find a plant that feasts on living things, on *flesh* beautiful," I said, and he chuckled as we made our way back outside leaving the mugginess of the glasshouse behind.

"Nearly all plants do however eat dead animals, and that includes humans my dear. They just do it with their roots where it is out of sight and out of mind. We Darlingtons like our little hobbies, just wait until Claude shows you his!"

As we walked back to join the rest of the family, I thought about what Lord Darlington had said, about Claude having a hobby. Claude had never mentioned anything but I know that men need their pursuits, and as wives we are expected to tolerate them, all the while keeping hold of the reins to prevent hobbies stealing our loved ones away.

We stayed in the garden for the remainder of the afternoon, returning inside in time for dinner just after the sky had darkened and light rain began to spot. I was right to assume that dinner was an equally lavish affair and I wondered how they managed to find the room or the appetite after such a generous lunch earlier. Later, we all retired to a charming informal sitting room, or music room for it had a large grand piano and a smaller harpsichord upon which Viola had seated herself and was playing a melodic yet unsophisticated tune. The harpsichord was a delight to behold with its decorative gilt work and beautiful soundboard decoration and I was informed by Dorothea, of its Italian origins and that it was an original piece from the Hall's early days. It gave a pleasing sound; the light jingly tones of the instrument were rich and more sonorous than any piano could be.

My eyes were growing heavy as I looked at the timepiece on the fireplace mantle; it was a full eleven-of-the clock. I looked to Claude and was about to make my excuses and retire to our bedchamber when Dorothea spoke.

"Arabella, I thought you should know, I've taken the liberty of making the necessary arrangements of hiring a lady's maid on your behalf. The service bureau will be sending the hopefuls to us tomorrow when my housekeeper, Mrs Dexter will conduct the necessary interviews. I think it might be a good idea if you were present, you can then choose whichever one is the more amiable."

I wasn't expecting such an appointment but before I could answer, the harpsichord was silenced abruptly with almost a clatter of noise. Viola stood from her stool and walked over to where Dorothea and I sat; she regarded us both through eyes that resembled blue slices. I now looked at her properly for the first time. She had plain features with a strong chin yet overall, she had a feminine build. Her hair was thick, straight, and yellow and she wore it in an elegant precise style. She stood shorter than I and she had long fingered hands which she clenched and unclenched as she stood poised wearing a vehement expression. Viola addressed her mother in a haughty manner.

"Mama, surely it is I who should procure a maid and not Arabella, who after all has only just arrived at Star Lake?" she spat with fury.

"My dearest Viola, you and I both share Nellie, it has always been our way. I thought you and Nellie got on rather well."

"We do but I think the time has come for me to have a maid of my own. I am a grown woman Mama!"

"Indeed you are my dear, but I could not expect Nellie to take care of all three of us, the poor girl would be wearied. With Arabella being the wife of your brother, who is the heir to Star Lake, it is the proper thing to do; I'm sure you understand dear."

"First it was my room that I had to relinquish, and now my turn for a maid, this really is unfair."

I suddenly realised one of the reasons behind Viola's dislike of me. It must have been her bed-chamber that Claude and I now occupied. She was younger than Claude, almost a woman but still a girl and perhaps it had been her room since leaving the nursery. I felt pangs of guilt that I had inadvertently upset Viola's plans at the Hall, putting her nose out of joint and ultimately hurting her feelings.

"Your mother is right Viola, let's hear no more of this," said Lord Darlington.

"We can talk about this in the morning dear, please play some more for us," said Dorothea, with a calmative tone.

"I shall not Mama!" Viola barked, and then she sat down in a chair near to the inert fireplace, and with folded arms she smouldered.

"You are acting like a spoilt princess again Viola, it is embarrassing," added Claude.

"I do not care. I am too cross to play."

"In that case, would my dearest Bella play for us? She has a great talent with the piano."

Claude's request caused Viola to seethe further, and I had no wish to add to her woes.

"Oh, no, I am rather tired," I said feigning a yawn.

"Oh, please do Bella, we would love to hear you play," said Dorothea, and both faces were filled with such expectation, that I could not find it within me to disappoint them. Carefully I seated myself at the piano and studied the music book resting upon the rack. The scores were all familiar to me but they were somewhat sombre, and I had a desire to lift the atmosphere with something light and cheerful. I began to play from memory and chose a simple Minuet dance melody but as I began to play Viola stood and with a shrill howl, she stomped out of the room with her arms rigid by her sides and hands screwed into fists.

"I am sorry," I said, and removed myself from the piano. "Perhaps she will feel better in the morning?" I added, referring to Viola's temper.

"Indeed, as I'm sure we all will," said Lord Darlington as he glanced at the clock.

"It is late my dear," he said, addressing Dorothea, "I think I shall go to bed. Will you join me?" Dorothea nodded and I took Claude's hand and soon we had all left the room and were climbing the stairs to the upper house.

That night as I lay in Claude's arms there was a bright moon that shone past the drapes and a solitary candle which burned low near the window. I watched the moths flutter against the casement glass until sleep came for me, and somewhere within my dreams I heard the haunting notes of an old Christian cradle song being played out from a harpsichord.

Chapter III
The lonely garden

Claude and I were first to rise, and we took breakfast and I remarked on Viola's apparent dislike of me. Claude dismissed my concerns saying: 'She has always been the jealous kind, and a little spiteful', and that I should simply ignore her as she would eventually concede. Despite what he said, I told him that I would endeavour to put things right with my sister-in-law; I still felt partly to blame for her unhappiness. Claude and I parted company early as we both had undertakings to fulfil. He had some work or other to carry out regarding a recently built structure at the Hall, the nature of which I gathered would be revealed to me shortly. I however had an engagement with the housekeeper, Mrs Dexter to interview for a maidservant.

I had no idea where I was to find Mrs Dexter that morning, so I sat in the library and waited to be called upon. The library was a spectacular room and was shelved floor to ceiling in a deep and rich flame mahogany, almost the colour of blood. The room housed the largest collection of books I had ever seen outside of a public library. Marble busts in the classical style were set atop each bookcase, and each bay of shelving had collections of established authors with their names painted onto the pelmets above. The books were ordered in neat rows so that their leather spines, all diverse in colour and shade, aligned perfectly. The gilded titles written on the spines glittered in the early morning light, it was as though I was looking at a patchwork blanket of words.

My fingers lightly stroked the books as I deliberated and finally, I decided upon a small red leather book, a collection of poetry by the romantic poet William Wordsworth. The library dovetailed neatly onto an adjoining conservatory where inside, nestled amongst the plants, I sat at a small reading table. No sooner had I opened the book when a small notelet fell into my lap. I placed the book, still open, face down upon the table and handled the note. It was a single piece of paper folded and upon which was written the following:

'*I have found it. I should not have entered, as I fear that my soul will forever be lost to it. She called to me again last night.*'

I had no idea what these words could mean or who could have written them, or even when. Perhaps, whoever wrote them was simply recording a favourite excerpt from the book. It was a trifle, and of no significance, yet for some reason I was drawn to the closing words: '*She called to me again last night.*' I felt a sensation of spider feet down my spine as I wondered who *she* was.

Dorothea suddenly appeared in the conservatory; she had been looking for me.

"Oh, Mrs Dexter is waiting for you in the housekeeper's room, which is just off the servant's hall, but it occurred to me that you would not know how to get there. I shall take you to her directly."

I thanked her and placed the notelet back into the book between the pages it had marked; it was a poem titled: '*It is no Spirit who from heaven hath flown.*' Dorothea noticed the book as I closed it. "That was Laurence's favourite book!" she said in surprise, looking at the book in my hand.

"Laurence?"

"Yes, Henry's brother. He loved to read that book. Always had it with him."

"I did not know Henry had a brother."

"Yes, a most unfortunate business but never mind. Pray follow me dear, you must choose your new maid."

Dorothea escorted me out of the conservatory, and I followed gripping the little red book tightly.

I sat next to Mrs Dexter as she *interrogated* the young woman who stood awkwardly and somewhat fearfully in front of her desk. Mrs Dexter was a mature woman whose silver hair was drawn back precisely into a tight bun. She always spoke with a strict voice as though she were a schoolmistress scolding a pupil. She was quite a forbidding person, and the poor girl who had come for the maidservant job quailed under her questioning.

The girl's name was Kitty (short for Katherine), she was slightly built and stood about five feet two inches tall. She had pale cream skin and hair the colour of red bricks. She spoke with an Irish accent. She had cool, yet friendly green eyes and wore a simple, yet perfectly pressed dress which after Mrs Dexter questioned her upon her ability as a seamstress, she disclosed that she had made herself. Mrs Dexter listened to Kitty's replies always with a perpetually raised eyebrow. I thought she had answered all the questions faultlessly and was easy to like and I had made my choice without having to see any other contenders.

Kitty was ushered away and asked to wait in the servant's kitchen whilst Mrs Dexter and I discussed her qualities. I made it clear I was happy with Kitty but Mrs Dexter did not want to appoint a maid without more than one choice of applicant. I asked if the salary being offered was less than in other big houses in the area, because I was expecting such a grand house to be a draw for those interested in a career in domestic service.

"On the contrary, the wages at Star Lake Hall exceed that which is paid in other houses," she said proudly.

"Then I wonder why we only have one potential maid here today?" I said.

Mrs Dexter, still with a raised eyebrow replied, "It is all nonsense you understand but this house has a … reputation; it is unfair, but the locals are a superstitious lot, and they never forget."

I pressed her to expand on her assertion about a reputation.

"It is nothing you need worry about. It all happened a very long time ago. All houses have a past but sometimes the past remains unforgotten. It leaves traces and marks and if you look for them you will find them, but it is all tomfoolery, this talk of ghosts."

"Ghosts!" I exclaimed.

"I have said more than I have a care to but if you would, take a leaf out of my book and pay no mind to such feather-brained talk," she finished, and I could see that no amount of any further pressing from me would force her to expand on the things she had merely touched upon. '*Ghosts.*' It was almost as though there was a mystery at Star Lake Hall, a mystery that perhaps could be linked to the dreams I always had about the place. I knew that I had the rest of my life to explore the secrecies surrounding the Hall's alleged reputation and I decided that I would begin by asking Claude.

Mrs Dexter and I both sat for another full hour without the arrival of any further applicants. Eventually, she capitulated and following another positive review of Kitty from me, we both agreed we should give her the good news. We found her still in the servant's kitchen drinking tea and chatting to a scullery maid; she was grateful for the offer and yet not overly delighted.

Mrs Dexter instructed Kitty to buy the appropriate apparel from a specified maker in the next town and that she should charge all expenses to Star Lake Hall. She was told that her employment would commence the next Monday and was then given a quick briefing on what her duties to me would be; such tasks as assisting me with my appearance including my makeup, hairdressing, clothing, jewellery and shoes. She would be required to remove stains from my clothes, sew, mend and alter garments when needed, bring me breakfast in bed and draw me a bath; all of which seemed excessive as I was unaccustomed to this level of attentiveness. I thought I would set out my own schedule which would I trust, be less demanding on Kitty whom I hoped would become more of a companion and friend during my time at Star Lake.

***

During the afternoon I decided to take a stroll outside around the grounds of the Hall. Claude had simply vanished; he had not appeared for luncheon with the rest of the family. Lord Darlington said that he was probably engrossed in his 'usual diversion', and I began to wonder if all days would be like this, with Claude missing and occupied in whatever pursuit had hold of him, whilst I, like a lost soul, was left to wander about Star Lake Hall in search of things to occupy my days or answers to mysteries that thus far had only been blithely revealed.

My meanderings took me through the walled garden where I had previously walked with Lord Darlington. I went along the underpass of verdant trees again and out into the wild and somewhat desolate patch where over to my left I could see again the gathering of gnarled and naked trees, aged and fragile, obscuring the summerhouse that sat within their midst. The afternoon had thus far been overcast but the grey was clearing, and only a few clouds now remained like garlands and rags to clutter the firmament. The sun emerged once again, and it was as if the day had opened wide and the sunlight had become a doorway into a dreamworld.

I wanted to sit here and capture the scene with my watercolours and decided I should do so perhaps tomorrow, providing the weather remained fine and dry. I was about to turn back when I heard something, a voice – no, laughter. A child's laugh, hollow but resonating. It appeared to come from the centre of the dead trees. Intrigued, I went over and as I did, I remembered the warnings from my father-in-law as he described the dangers of the unstable trees and the foot-hooking roots: '*Viola had an accident there as a child*,' his words stayed with me as I approached the summerhouse. The area was a knot of stubborn bramble and lichen freckled bark.

The once brightly painted shelter was now a neglected hut throttled by barbed climbers, and vines partly obscured the doorway but not fully and I was able to carefully squeeze inside. I do not know what possessed me to enter the structure, but I thought I could hear whispers. The ghosts of voices mingled with the soft trills of birds as they darted between the thorns and passed in and out of the summerhouse through the remnants of the glass windows now darkened by mildew, vine and creeper. A sense of loneliness stole over me with only the sound of my own feet as they crunched upon old, dried leaves and twigs.

I saw the same figure of a man in a window between the central gables, almost a silhouette, motionless, so very far away from me yet I had the feeling I was constantly under his gaze.

I heard the laughter again only this time from outside and it was as though a shadow fell over the doorway and it frightened me because I was alone and nothing else was here, nothing that could cast a shadow. I leapt outside scratching my arm on the teethlike thorns that grew upon the rigid curtain that partly covered the doorway. I was breathing quickly, and my heart was rattled but the warm sunlight calmed me as I stood bathed in its protective light. I recovered myself and as I stepped away from the summerhouse, I saw a china doll lying within the unmown tussocks. I stood over it, I had not noticed the doll on my way over and yet the grass was flattened as though it had only recently been placed upon it. I picked up the doll and although it had been bathed in the strong sunlight it felt cold as though it had been made from snow. The doll's pale face was covered in a spiderweb of timeworn cracks, yet its eyes were so blue and unblemished, staring at me endlessly, and its hands with missing fingers now resembled claws.

I dropped the doll and lifted my gaze to Star Lake Hall. The house, being so large and pervasive, was always in sight from the gardens and grounds. I saw the same figure of the man in a window between the central gables, almost a silhouette, motionless, so very far away from me yet I had the feeling I was constantly under his gaze. My heart began to drum in my breast, and I was relieved to hear a familiar voice calling for me. I turned to see Claude emerge from the tunnel of branch and leaves and I called over to him. I suspect that my voice quavered under my scare as he came running and whilst I waited for him, I turned to look once more to the form at the window, but it was gone, *he*, was gone, and more inexplicable was the fact the window also seemed to have vanished as though wiped off the face of the house. I searched again between the gables but there was only brick and no casement. I continued to search for the window; my eyes flitted around the façade, even upon the summit of the house where the chimney stacks reached heavenward into the golden sunlight. There was nothing.

Claude reached me and I embraced him with such a need for comfort.

"Bella, what is wrong, what has troubled you so?" he asked, as he beheld my face which I imagine must have looked paler than usual.

"The figure," I said pointing towards the house.

"Figure?"

"Yes, and, and the—" I pointed to a flattened tuft of grass, but the doll had also gone as though, like snow it had melted away to seep into the thirsting earth.

"Arabella? You are not making any sense."

Claude himself became fearful and I decided for now at least, not to worry him any further.

"I cut my arm," I said, and I showed him where the thorns had ripped my sleeve and the spots of red that had begun to bleed through the fabric.

"My goodness, we shall go back to the house at once, this wound needs attention."

"Please, do not mention this to your father, he told me not to wander into this part of the garden, he said it was unsafe. I do not want him to think I disregarded his advice," I pleaded.

Claude agreed and he carefully and attentively escorted me back to the house.

Claude took me through the vacuous ballroom to a powder room that was positioned opposite a gentlemen's restroom. We were quite alone, and he disappeared to go and fetch some ointment and a cloth to clean my wounds. As I waited, I stepped outside of the powder room and took in the opulence and splendour of the enormous ballroom. In this sumptuous state it was a far cry from the ice-covered space I had often visited in my dreams.

Although presently unused, the room had been kept in the most pristine condition with enormous glittering chandeliers and beautiful furniture covered with white sheets of linen. The wrappings themselves reawakened visions of the barren, frozen room where the linen coverlets would be replaced with snow, deep and untouched, and the faceted crystal drops of the chandeliers shattered and ruined by the wind and gripped by unsightly twisted stalactites of ice. I shivered as I remembered the pensive visions but the sound of Claude's footsteps echoing upon the marble flooring as he came back for me cleared away these thoughts, as though they were merely breaths upon a mirror.

As Claude dabbed at my arm with a cloth, I asked him about the house's '*reputation.*'

"What reputation?" he queried, whilst engrossed in cleaning my wounds.

"It is just something Mrs Dexter said this morning. She spoke of Star Lake Hall having a past and she even mentioned *ghosts!*"

"Ghosts!" laughed Claude, "there are no ghosts Bella, just stories that keep those foolish enough to believe such things awake at night and fearful of their own shadows."

"What stories?"

"Silly things my darling, silly impossible stories, and nothing to worry about."

It was almost as though he did not want to talk about it, to think of it even but I wanted to know what everyone knew; I did not want to be the only one oblivious to it all.

"What happened to your uncle?" I asked, and he stopped attending to my arm to stare at me with a puzzled look.

"Who?"

"Laurence, your uncle. Your mother mentioned him today."

Claude replaced the cap on the ointment and began to bind my arm with a light dressing.

"I don't know, for sure. You see Bella, my uncle disappeared. I don't … we don't know what became of him."

"How did he disappear? Did he simply leave Star Lake?"

"It was before my time Bella. My parents were both still young and only recently wed."

He finished the bandaging and gently lowered my sleeve.

"You must know something about it, a story perhaps?" I persisted.

"There you go again; you must not believe all the stories you hear Bella."

"I have not heard anything, that is why I ask you of it."

He kissed my hand and breathed out a sigh of surrender.

"It was Christmas Eve, the family were all in the drawing room, it was a tradition for them to exchange a gift before the clock struck midnight, but my uncle was missing. Servants were sent off to look for him whilst the family waited. The account, as I have known it, was that Uncle Laurence had been ill at ease with himself the whole day, and for many days before. It was as though he had become obsessed with finding *something* within the house. According to Mother he would be found scrutinising old plans of the house, sometimes until the early hours of the morning. The lack of sleep became quite detrimental to his health and his faculties, and he became quite sick. Mother spoke about how she watched him turn from a vigorous, robust man into a pale shadow of himself within weeks as his mania took possession of him. All I know then is that after a fruitless search of the house that Christmas Eve, they could not find him, and they never saw anything of him again."

"What do you think happened to him?" I asked, as it seemed implausible that a man could simply vanish as Laurence was supposed to have done.

"I do not know Bella. According to Baxter, who was then underbutler at the house, they dredged the lakes and searched the grounds exhaustively.

He had left no trace of departure from the house; all the horses were in their stables and his money and clothes were still in his room. He was my father's older brother and the rightful heir to Star Lake Hall, so the searches continued for years until finally it was presumed, he had been somehow abducted by nefarious means. My father always spoke of how he had had associations with dangerous men with whom he became acquainted through various spheres of interest. Obviously, everything could have been all so different for us if it had not happened. Someday I shall inherit the house and with you by my side."

Claude finished relating the story as how he knew it to be. I did not press him any further even though I felt he still knew more than he told because it was clear he did not feel comfortable speaking of it; sometimes it is best to leave ghosts in the past where they belong. I had wondered why Claude was in the garden when he found me amongst the dead trees, so I asked him.

"I was looking for you my dear, because I have a little surprise for you."

He took up my hand, "There is something I want to show you, come!"

I was led up to where our bedchamber sat amongst the unused nursey and other family rooms. He guided me to a door that was flanking the nursery and with a broad smile he opened it. The room beyond was bright and aired and there was a garden-fresh smell from a vase of pink and yellow roses all in unspoilt bloom. There was an assortment of tables, and cabinets and cubby-holes, and near to the window stood an artist's easel, and by its side a table stacked with sketch books, papers and painting canvas. Claude reached up to a cabinet and lifted down a hinged wooden box and presented me with it. He bade me to open it and I have never in my life seen such a fine assortment of artists brushes, and paints, and nibs.

"I know how much you love to paint, and I thought you would need an artist's room. It is your room Bella, I arranged it myself and tried to think of all the articles that you would need."

I was both surprised and delighted that my dearest Claude had been so thoughtful, knowing how much I loved to paint and how this room all my own would help me to feel more at home here.

"Think of it as a little early birthday present," he said.

After all that had happened lately, the wedding, and honeymoon and arrival at the house, my own birthday had quite slipped my mind.

"There is something else Bella, I spoke with Mother this morning and we shall mark the forthcoming celebration with a party at the Hall; you must invite your parents, it will be a joyous occasion!"

Claude's face beamed with delight as he gave me his news. I have never been one to enjoy attention and the prospect of a party in my honour I confess, filled me with some discomfiture but it would be lovely to see my mother and father again after so many weeks apart.

"I expect you will want a new gown for the party. You can leave that expense to me my darling," he added.

I suddenly had so many new things to think of - my new life at Star Lake, a new maid, my very own artist's room, and now, what undoubtedly would be a lavish party in no less than three weeks. I was glad of these distractions as there had grown a persistent shadow that now crept along with my thoughts since I had arrived at the house.

***

Another evening slipped by and as we sat in the drawing room, I thought about the story Claude had told me earlier. I pictured his parents as a young married couple sat either side of a thriving winter fire holding unwrapped gifts on their laps. I thought about his uncle Laurence, and how the house must have been a hive of activity as the searches were conducted. Yet now all was quiet as the stillness of another almost airless summer night seeped into the bricks of the house, and the moonlight painted a lattice upon the walls as it shone through the unveiled windows.

Viola sat and played *whist* with Dorothea. Lord Darlington was asleep in his chair with a port on a table at his elbow and a book of botany resting against his chest was slowly slipping from his fingers. Claude as usual had been stolen away by his mysterious hobby. I sat with my book – *Laurence's book* – and I read Wordsworth's poem that Laurence had marked with his notelet, where he had underscored the words: '*My soul an Apparition in the place, tread there with steps that no one shall reprove!*' I wondered why these words were significant enough for him to mark them in the book that had become to him a dear friend, a book that perhaps fate had guided my hand to pick out.

In the still of the room, I had become aware of the grandfather clock ticking, the ticking away of the days of our lives as the quantity of times past increased. Only during peace and quietude does one become aware of the rhythmic marking of time. The clock suddenly sprang into voice as the quarter-hour was reached. Lord Darlington woke from his slumber and rubbed his eyes as he glanced at the clock's resplendent face. Dorothea and Viola became almost frozen in time as they both sat poised, listening to the familiar chimes.

A door opened and Claude entered. He came to me and kissed my cheek.

"I know you must wonder why I have left you alone most evenings since our return from Venice, now I would like to show you the reason."

"Oh, but the hour is late my love," I said.

"It is the perfect time, and the only time that I can show you during these summer months."

The others did not seem to notice as Claude and I slipped from the room.

After rising to the upper floor, we travelled from one end of Star Lake to the other and climbed a stone stairwell that spiralled up to a single door. The room beyond took my breath away. I was expecting some gloomy gothic turret covered in dust and the lacework of spiders, yet this space was an inviting chamber. Candles burned brightly from wall-mounted sconces, and there was even a bed in the corner. I imagined how snug the room could be even in winter with bright bouncing flames held captive within the small fireplace near to the bed. Under the candlelight a myriad of contraptions sparkled, and I had no notion as to the purpose of all the apparatus and machines within. I looked to Claude for an explanation.

"Welcome to my observatory Bella!" he said, and he began turning a wheel attached to a set of gears and cogs and the roof began to open as one part slid under the other creating a wide slot. Almost breathless with zeal I watched as he removed a heavy sheet from what I could now see was a telescope but much larger than any I had seen before. He rotated the device and tilted it so that its far end pointed towards the gap in the roof, and he pressed his eye to the nearest end that narrowed and tapered into an eyepiece.

I stood still and watched patiently as he made some adjustments to his instrument and then he called me over.

"Bella, please look," he said, and he helped me to correctly place my eye to the instrument and I then saw a glaring globe that I first mistook to be the moon, our worlds constant companion but then I saw the tawney-coloured bands and a string of lights almost like a necklace of stars.

"It's beautiful. What is it?"

"You are observing Jupiter my dearest Bella, the Queen of the planets."

"What are the jewels that are suspended near?"

"They are her moons Bella."

In disbelief, I placed my eye against the telescope once more and as I peered, I could even make out the tiny crescents.

"Do you mean to say that there are other moons in the sky?"

In all my life I had only thought of the moon as a solitary body; the idea that more may litter the firmament was to me at least, somewhat of a revelation.

"There are, and so many other wondrous things that the dark heavens keep secret from us but now I, like other men, are beginning to unlock the mysteries of the skies."

"Then this is what you do, you explore the heavens with your devices? For what purpose my love?"

"To be the first Bella, the first to discover new worlds, new suns."

"Suns?"

First Claude had surprised me with his talk of a multitude of moons but was he now seriously expecting me to accept that we had more than one sun in the sky?

"Take a look heavenwards, what do you see?" he said, and pointed with a long arm upwards to the slot in the roof.

"I see the stars, twinkling like little diamonds, why, what do you see?"

"Those sparkling specks that pepper the night sky are the echoes of ancient suns Bella, suns not unlike our own, and perhaps with their own worlds bound to them, a home for people just like us. People doing what we are doing now, looking outwards at the stars; perhaps they are seeing our star, our sun but as it once was, perhaps at the dawn of time."

I had never thought about the nature of the stars that speckled the darkness above, I had just accepted them as one accepts clouds and rainbows and other constant worldly things. I never questioned it, until now.

"Do you hope to find more worlds? Do you think you can?" I said, as I began to understand Claude's enchantment by the magic of it all.

"I do, and my telescope was constructed by the finest makers in Switzerland, and I have spared no expense creating a place in which to put it."

He spun around with his arms outspread as though to illustrate the excellence of the observatory. "Living in a house called Star Lake Hall, how could I not be drawn to the stars that sprinkle the sky above it. I feel as though somehow, I have been called to the stars, to this inky blackness as though it is my destiny."

He stopped and held me in his gaze without looking away and I became lost in his adorable blue eyes as he embraced me, drawing me close to him.

"It was my destiny also to find you dearest Arabella, my love, with beauty beyond all others and with hair as dark as the midnight sky itself, and like the stars above us, you have been made wholly to be loved."

We made love in the observatory that wonderful July night, and afterwards we lay in each other's arms with the roof open to the heavens. We lay still in the peace that comes from within a lover's embrace. Claude pointed to a pair of stars that stood out brightly in the night sky.

"You see the twin stars Bella, that is us and whenever you look up there, we shall be, you and I side by side in perpetuity. Remember it always."

Chapter IV
The unwanted gift.

There are only five of us in residence at Star Lake Hall but with the house being a sizeable one there is still a need for a large body of servitorial staff and many were becoming familiar to me. Initially I had only encountered Mr Baxter and Mrs Dexter as most of the other staff were like shadows, carrying out their work in an inconspicuous manner but now I had become acquainted with the footmen Archie and Leo, Lord Darlington's valet Hugh, Claude's valet Fergus, and Dorothea and Viola's maid Nellie. My own maid, Kitty was due to start the following morning. I was looking ahead to the prospect of having another woman with whom I could converse and perhaps even confide in, especially regarding matters I did not want to speak of with Claude, or the rest of the family.

Claude for a while had closed the door to his tower and window to the stars and had been more of a presence around the place but today was Sunday and he had taken to his turret with renewed

interest, following the delivery from Switzerland
the previous day of a new lens, a lens that he said
would enable him to increase the size of the ob-
jects viewed down his telescope.

Without much to do I had taken my easel and
paints outside during the morning, where I sat
and tried to capture the moment when the fresh
sunlight of a new day unwraps the colours of the
garden. Afterwards, in the ensuing torpor of that
warm, unemployed afternoon I went to the drawing room and sat to read. I took with me the red
book of poetry that had once belonged to Claude's
Uncle Laurence, and as I flicked through the fine
delicate pages, I found to my surprise a dried ivy
leaf that had been pressed inside.

The aged leaf was now almost transparent save
for its delicate veins and it still retained its fragile stalk. I wondered why it had been kept in the
book and preserved like a keepsake of fondness.
As I held the leaf I watched with amazement as it
began to crumble before my eyes and in less than
mere seconds it had become reduced to a fine dust
upon my palm. It was almost as though the leaf itself had remembered that it was only ever meant
to be a short-lived relic from long ago and the air
in the room and the breath from my lungs had
sparked the process of decay. I blew the dust from
my hand and saw that the leaf had in fact left the
ghost of an imprint, the only reminder that it had
ever existed at all within the book that had for so

very long sheltered and protected it.

Lord Darlington came into the room followed by Hugh, his valet. I overheard the pair of them discussing the whereabouts of Darlington's spectacles which he had misplaced. I watched as they searched and then Hugh discovered them behind a cushion on Darlington's favourite armchair. Relieved to have found them at last he thanked Hugh sending him on his way to other matters then he turned his attention on to me, and particularly the book I had placed on my lap. He asked how I had managed to find it as though it, like his spectacles, had somehow become lost.

"I chose it from a bookcase in the library," I explained.

"It was my brother's favourite book; if you don't mind I would very much like to have it," he said, and he held out his hand in anticipation. Reluctantly I offered him the book which he only glanced at before slipping it inside his waistcoat. He smiled at me before fetching himself a drink from a decanter upon a small side table. I declined the offer of one myself and he returned to where I sat. He took a sip from his glass before speaking again.

"It has been a great pleasure having you come to live at Star Lake Arabella, and I will not ask many things of you, except for one."

I was now intrigued as to the nature of his impending request, and I waited in suspense to hear of it.

"Please promise that you will not go poking around the house, exploring, looking for secret doors to secret rooms that frankly do not exist."

When he finished speaking, he gazed at me awaiting a response. I had no notion at all of what these concerns of his were, so I nodded.

"Of course. I do promise," I simply said.

"Good, I know that it may sound silly … what I ask of you, and please don't ask me to explain my motives, because I would be unable to do so with any rationality."

He placed his drink down and then he removed the little red book from his waistcoat turning it over in his hands as he studied it.

"It was just seeing you with my brother's book, it rekindled the memories. He was a troubled man. I don't suppose you know the story at all."

"I have heard a little … from Claude," I added. He seemed surprised I knew anything at all about his brother's disappearance. He glanced towards the window where the sun was shining with vigour and spilling through, highlighting all the articles within the room.

"Anyway, let's not dwell on the past. I expect you are looking forward to the party," he said, changing the subject.

"Yes, I am, and thank you. It will be good to see my parents again."

"Yes, it will, I expect you miss them. I hope you are not too lonely here with Claude spending so much time in his observatory."

"No, it's quite alright, I do have my painting and—"

"Yes well, nevertheless, I shall have a word with him my dear. I do not want you to feel you are imprisoned at Star Lake, you can visit your family anytime you wish. You may take one of the coaches; just let me know and I will inform Watson, our driver."

"Thank you, I expect that I shall."

"Good, now I must go and talk to the gardener, it is high time he sorted out those dead trees before the winter sets in. It is quite exposed here, and the wind can be jolly fierce!"

Lord Darlington left me in the drawing room where I sat alone and now bereft of the little book that had so intrigued me. As I sat in the stillness of the afternoon, I pondered about what he had said regarding looking for secret rooms.

The following morning, first thing after breakfast, Kitty was escorted to see me by Mrs Dexter. She was wearing a print gown over which was a white linen apron pinned to her bodice. Her red hair was neatly tamed under a simple white cap.

"Good morning m'lady," she said politely.

Mrs Dexter then bade her to go and make up our bedchamber and she dutifully set off to do so. Once Mrs Dexter had returned to her own burdens, I joined Kitty in my bedchamber and greeted her less formally now that we were both out from under Mrs Dexter's stern gaze.

We talked about Star Lake Hall, and I remarked how like her I was also new to the house being recently married to Claude and then taking up residence. She said that she had always desired to work at such a grand place, but that Star Lake was her least preferred option. She had in fact answered the job advert only after being refused a position at other nearby country houses due to the Masters' partiality about her '*Irishness*.' I asked Kitty why Star Lake had been such a poor choice for her.

"I shouldn't say but 'twas me father, 'e said de place is cursed!" she said sheepishly, in her appealing accent.

"Cursed? Why would he think that about the house?"

"It's a well-known story around 'ere, dat once in a while de 'ouse takes folks. Me father was worried about me."

Kitty blushed, for she was obviously embarrassed to be talking to me about these matters, and I felt guilty at drawing this out from her, especially as this was her first day at the house, but my curiosity was roused. My own family home was not so many miles away, yet I had not been exposed to the kind of stories that Kitty was alluding to. I wanted to learn more from her and perhaps it might even explain what happened to Laurence.

"When you say that the house takes people,

what do you mean?"

"Like I said, it takes folks, dey go missin' and are never seen again. Everyone from far and wide be scared to come near de place. Dey also say dat it is *haunted*."

Kitty suddenly looked very ashamed of what she had said.

"I'm sorry m'lady I shouldn't 'ave said anyt'eng. Please don't say I said anyt'eng especially to dat oder woman, Mrs Dexter. I need de job … my family needs de money."

I thanked Kitty for being so honest and assured her that I would say nothing to anyone else about what she had told me, and she seemed more at ease again afterwards. I then lightened the mood by talking to her about the forthcoming party and about the gown that was being made for me. I showed her an illustration and a sample of the material that the clothier had provided.

"Oh, you are going to look so beautiful m'lady, I can't wait to see you in it!" she said, with genuine delight.

***

The following few days passed relatively uneventfully. I felt much more settled and at home now at Star Lake than ever. With Claude's periodic absences and preoccupations within his observatory, I had taken to spending more time in my painting room where I had begun to paint scenes from my own imaginings, more specifically from my persistent dreams about a frozen Star Lake Hall that had dogged me for most of my life. For these images, I chose oils on canvas, and for what they lacked in colour (due to the predominant theme being an icy whiteness) they made up for in mood and tone alone. The paintings were somewhat bleak and sombre, and I had taken to try to capture the likenesses of many of the statuesque forms held in their anguished state of repose, half buried under the mantle of ice and snow. For obvious reasons I kept these paintings private and hidden for they were not as it were, for general concern, unlike my cheery watercolours of the grounds and the house which I had taken to hanging about the walls of my atelier.

There were some mornings when Claude would be absent, due to him rising before dawn and taking himself away, so that he could view and chart the seasonal celestial bodies that so often fascinated him. During these early mornings I would disappear off to my art chamber and continue with whatever was the current project upon the easel. I had done so one morning, and still in my nightwear, I had taken breakfast whilst I had sat to paint. Kitty knew where to find me on such early mornings for she had grown accustomed to my habits as I had to hers. As usual, after she had set my breakfast tray down, she remarked upon my paintings with honest appraisal. On this particular morning I was working on one of my dream-induced surrealistic scenes and I was unable to cover it before she entered the room and saw it.

I was embarrassed by the painting since it may itself have brushed *me* with a character assumed to be quite eccentric, if not fully soft-headed. She walked over to the easel and stared at the saturnine image before her.

"Oh, m'lady, what made you paint such a t'eng?"

She peered at the picture and recognised the twin staircase draped in ice.

"Why, it's Star Lake, but why is it so cold?"

"It is just a silly fancy of mine, nothing serious. I … I sometimes like to imagine things very differently to what they are," I said, trying to lessen the impact of what the depiction was trying to achieve.

"Oh, but de people m'lady, are dey … dead?"

I did not want to say any more about the painting, so I covered it over and took my breakfast tray.

"I'm sorry m'lady I did not wish to pry," Kitty said apologetically.

I was about to tell her not to worry but then I looked at her properly for the first time that morning and I could see that her face was troubled, and it had nothing to do with the painting, so I asked her about it, and she was forthcoming with her reply.

"It's Miss Viola m'lady, she's been giving me many errands and chores and it seems I can never please 'er enough, and ..."

"Go on Kitty, what else?"

"I don't like to say but she is quite unkind to me m'lady, de way she speaks to me. She calls me an *Oirish* biddy!"

I was shocked to hear of this apparent malice from Viola but not in the least surprised.

"Oh, Kitty, this will not do at all. I will have a word with Viola, I—"

"No please don't, I don't want to make any trouble worse."

"No, you must not suffer this ill-treatment, and besides, *Nellie* is Viola's maid not you."

"Oh, I wish I had said not'eng now, it will be a lot of trouble. I shouldn't 'ave opened my big mouth!"

"Nonsense, I am glad you told me Kitty. but I promise I will not make any more trouble for you. Leave it with me for now but please be sincere and tell me of any further bother."

"Thank you m'lady," she said, and her eyes misted with tears as she left my company.

***

It was the morning of my twenty fourth birthday. I felt like my day had bloomed beautifully as Claude had spent the whole night in our bed and his breaths, as he slept by my side had brought a calmness to my mind and dreams, almost as does a soothing lullaby. I could see the morning trying to squeeze past the folds of the heavy drapes and I hoped that this particular one had brought with it a sense of all the old spirits of nature braiding together; all that is heavenly and good and that it would wipe away everything that had so far attempted to irk me during my early weeks at Star Lake Hall.

We took breakfast in bed; Kitty had placed a fresh cut flower in a delicate posy vase, and she presented me with a small gift of a beautifully hand-embroidered handkerchief. It was a delightful present and so good of her to think of me. Fergus arrived with Claude's tray and newspaper, and we were then left alone to our eggs and toast and tea and embraces before being dressed for the morning. Kitty fashioned my hair and was excited at the prospect of later having the task with helping me into my evening wear for the party that was to commence at eight-of-the clock. My own excitement however was induced by the pleasant thought of being reunited with my parents who I had missed so dearly; for me the time couldn't pass quickly enough.

Claude and I entered the morning room to find that the rest of the family were already present. Lord Darlington, who I have now come to call Henry, was standing beside Dorothea and they greeted me affectionately and even Viola offered me a polite reception, although still somewhat reserved.

"You must open your presents dear," cried Dorothea, and she took my arm and steered me over to a lamp table upon which was assembled a collection of gifts wrapped in lustrous paper with the kind of shiny ribbons and bows that I would use to adorn my hair or even a bonnet.

"Open ours, I do hope you like it!" said Dorothea enthusiastically.

She handed me a weighty article and I unwrapped its outer skin of pearlescent paper to reveal a jewellery casket in polished, bevelled cobalt blue glass and beautifully decorated in silver and enamel. I placed the box down on the table using the two silver-hinged handles and opened the lid. The daylight immediately flooded inside, and the box was illuminated almost magically. It was a beautiful object and I thanked both Dorothea and Henry warmly.

"There's another part," said Henry, and he pointed to an extra package lying flat on the table.

Once unwrapped I saw a set of jewelled hat pins that looked so exquisite and ever so expensive.

"Oh, they are lovely, you spoil me too much," I said.

"Nonsense, if we cannot spoil you on your birthday, then when can we my dear!" boomed Henry.

"Oh, but the party tonight, all that expense just

for me, I simply do not know what to say."

Viola ejected a scornful snort at my words.

"You do not have to say anything my dear. You are one of the family, and this is how we do things here, at Star Lake Hall," replied Dorothea before Viola reached over to the table and retrieved a small neatly wrapped parcel.

"Here, I hope you like it," she said, handing me the bundle. I opened it to find a collection of scented soaps. I thanked her and she smiled what I felt to be a faux smile before she took a seat by the window and diverted her gaze once more out into the gardens.

Claude then reached over to the table and picked up a large flat square parcel and handed it to me. "This is from me my love," he said, and I tore off the paper wrappings and opened the lid on the rectangular box that my nails had uncovered, and inside was the most beautiful necklace that I had ever seen. The diamonds shimmered just as the stars had that night under the unlocked roof of the observatory. The whole band glittered as I turned it in my hands. I saw Dorothea place a hand to her chest in admiration of it.

"Oh, Claude," I said but no more words would come, for I was in wonder and awe of this beautiful gift.

"Let me," said Claude, and he took the necklet from my hands and gently secured it upon me,

DAVID RALPH WILLIAMS

and I could feel the coolness of it as it lay against my skin.

"It is the wearer of the jewels who is the real beauty, the one true star beneath the black skies." For a moment I was lost in Claude's poetic words, that adorable man who holds my heart in his endless blue eyes.

"There appears to be another gift," Henry said, scratching his head. "Funny, I do not remember seeing it there just a moment ago."

I looked down at the table and near to the base of the inert lamp was indeed another parcel. This one was not so richly covered for it did not have the curling opulent bows and ties; instead, a twine of ivy had been secured around it and knotted carefully so as not to break the stem. I picked the parcel up and looked at Claude for an explanation.

"Not from me I am afraid," was his answer.

"Or from us dear," added Dorothea.

The package felt cold to the touch, and as I undid the wrappings, I half expected to find within it a hunk of ice.

When the last of the paper was removed, I was confronted by the same doll I had discovered in the garden that day when Claude had found me frightened and bleeding amongst the dead trees. The same white porcelain face marred by a mapwork of fine fractures. The lidless eyes, the ceaseless gape. The toy had the propensity to attest to all my hidden superstitious terrors. My hands

70

trembled as I held the doll, and I was unable to keep hold of the thing; I dropped it. Henry quickly scooped it up and in one single sweep of his arm he cast it into the cold grate of the fireplace. He then picked up a fire hook and used it to smash the doll. I could hear how the china was broken into what must have been a thousand gleaming *icy* fragments to lie sharp and vicious within the iron grille. I had a vision that were I to peer over Henry's stooping shoulder I might even see redness bleeding out from the slivers.

The lidless eyes, the ceaseless gape. The toy had the propensity to attest to all my hidden superstitious terrors.

I saw Dorothea's shocked face as she watched Henry in what could only be described as a 'moment of madness'. He finished his wreckage of the doll then wiped his brow and turned to face us.

"That ... thing. Who placed it there? Where *did*

you find it?" he said tensely, as he looked from one of us to the other. There was only silence because nobody I believe had even a splinter of an answer. After looking at all our mute faces, he turned to face Viola who still sat on the window seat wearing the same mask of shock as the rest of us.

"Was it you? Was this one of your nasty and spiteful little games?"

"Papa … I … no! Of course not!" Viola implored, then immediately she erupted into a flood of tears and darted out of the room in bursts of sobs. Dorothea looked at Henry for an explanation, but none was given. He then turned to look at me.

"I am very sorry my dear, please do not let this little upset spoil the rest of your day."

Henry walked over to where a tray of tea things had been placed and he poured himself a cup.

"Would anyone like some tea?" he said, feeling somewhat responsible for the dark atmosphere that had scarred the morning.

"I should go after Viola," replied Dorothea, before leaving the room. Claude sought an explanation from Henry about his odd behaviour and subsequent outburst at Viola. Henry gave none but continued to apologise for the disturbance and was so genuinely regretful that if Viola were still present, I think that she would have had to forgive him.

After lunch I took myself away to my atelier

where I sat amongst my paintings. I grew impatient with the hands on the clocks because I wanted the time before the arrival of my parents to pass swiftly like the clouds that now raced overhead as I looked out of the windows. A strong breeze had developed as the afternoon dawdled by and there was a distinct feeling during mid-afternoon as though there was somebody about the house more than there appeared to be. It seemed that only I noticed the atmospheres: merely shadows, and flickers just out of sight of the eyes. I thought I could perceive whispers distinct from the wails and the whines that were blowing down the chimneys.

That afternoon Viola had apparently hidden herself away in her bedchamber. I tried several times to speak with her as I thought it was about time that we made our peace, but she never answered my knocks upon her door or replied to my calls. During the last attempt I thought that I could hear sobbing and again I began to feel pangs of guilt that my arrival at Star Lake had caused her so much burden. I was about to walk away from her bedchamber when the door opened. I turned to find her standing in the doorway, her face still wet with tears.

"Yes?" she said simply.

"I just wanted to make sure that you were alright, after what happened this morning."

She just looked at me with her usual blank

emotionless face.

"I was concerned – am concerned," I continued. "I know you find it difficult, me being here and I am sorry, I truly am if I have done anything at all to cause you to dislike me so."

Viola dabbed at her misted blue eyes with a handkerchief as she listened to me. Her usual tidy hair was a jumble as though she had pulled at it with her hands. She pushed back the hair from her face like she was opening drapes.

"We are now family, and I have never had a sister before and I would very much like it if we could be friends," I finished, then looked past her and into her room and I saw a gown hanging from a clothes rail. It was a pretty dress fashioned in crimson silk. I remarked on how beautiful it was and was surprised when she then moved away from the doorframe to sit upon her bed to regard the dress.

"I am wearing it tonight at the party. Do you think red is too garish, only I wanted to catch the eyes of all the wealthy eligible bachelors, although, I expect that yours is much finer?" she remarked.

I took this as an invitation to enter her room; boldly I stepped through the open doorway.

Viola's room was very cluttered. The jumble consisted mostly of books and natural artefacts, notably shells and stones and the skulls of small animals. There was also a vast collection of childhood games, dolls, and knick-knacks, possessions she had accumulated during her lifetime. I noticed that she had various papier-mâché facemasks that I assumed she had made herself; some were beautifully crafted and decorated and I could see that she had inherited some of Dorothea's artistic abilities. With my own love for art, it was a good starting point for us to find some common ground.

I commented on her masks, notably her animal designs and elaborate masquerade eyeshades. I told her how clever and lovely they were and for a while we played as two young girls might do, wearing each mask in turn and Viola's whole temperament was elevated and it heartened me to see it. I noticed that there was one mask on a different hook to the others. I had never seen that mask before, yet its white almost cherubic face looked familiar. I removed it from its pin and noticed how Viola had painstakingly used a slender brush to create the illusion of fine fractures as found on broken china and to give the mask doll-like features, with wide blue eyes and cherry red lips.

Viola saw me with the mask, and she seized it from my hands and then hid it out of sight inside a low walnut cupboard.

She turned to me, "It was not I who wrapped the doll and left it with your other presents. It was the girl."

It seemed like an odd thing for her to suddenly

proclaim.

"Girl? What girl?" I asked, wondering who she meant.

"The girl who haunts the place. Oh, surely you must know that the house has a ghost!"

Chapter V
An indistinct room

"When I was a little girl, I used to help Papa with his carnivorous plants. Have you seen them?" asked Viola. I nodded to say I had, and she continued with her tale whilst we sat in her bedchamber. "Good, you see I used to like catching creepy-crawlies in the garden and then I would feed them to his plants. It seemed the best thing to do with the beastly things really. Once, I borrowed a trowel that the gardener had left in Papa's glasshouse, and I went off to dig up worms. I often played around the summerhouse that was almost concealed within a ring of old trees. Whilst I sat digging with my trowel, I thought I heard laughter, giggles really. I assumed that we had visitors at Star Lake. I thought perhaps my aunt and uncle from Norwich had come to visit Mama and had brought with them their bothersome little oik of a son, my cousin George. I stopped digging because the laughter was so annoying. I tried to ignore it at first but when it carried on insistently, I stopped what I was doing again and began to look for him, only it was not George but a girl about the same age as me or so I could tell."

As I sat and listened to Viola's story, I watched how her face began to change; gone was her sparkle which was now replaced with a frown. "I don't know how I knew her age because I could not see her properly, she was always in shadow and hid behind the trees, but we were the same height or thereabouts. I ran around the trees holding my trowel trying to scare her so she would appear and I could see her and find out what she was doing in *my* garden, but she was always so very quick, darting from one trunk to another. In the end I lost her, and I sat down on the grass frustrated at my failure. It was then I heard a noise from above and when I looked up, I thought I saw her high in one of the trees. She was shaking the branches and I heard a sharp crack, and a thick arm of the tree came loose. I tried to run but my foot became trapped under a tree root and before I knew it, I was buried under the branch. It broke my arm look!" She rolled up a sleeve to show me the silver streak of a scar running across her upper arm.

"Gracious! What happened next?" I asked, feeling the horror of what she had told me.

"I cried and screamed, and Papa found me, although I had lain under the branch for a long while. *She* sat in the tree all the time I lay there but she was quiet, just watching me, with the sun behind her so I could not see her face. When Papa arrived, she simply vanished, like a star behind a cloud. Almost everyone sees her sometimes, but they will never admit it. I know Mama sees her, and I suspect Baxter does also. He once tried to cover the windows with the drapes one evening early in winter as the sun was dipping behind the trees. He saw something I know he did, and he wanted to protect us … me, from also seeing it."

"What about Claude?" I asked, "Does he see her?"

"I doubt it. My brother thinks of himself as a great scientist who studies the heavens. I imagine the very idea of a ghost seems preposterous to him, yet they exist all the same."

I watched as she left the bed to wander over to the casement. She gazed out through the glass as she next spoke and I could see that from this vantage point, although some distance away, it was possible see the old summerhouse and the coil of brickly trees that fenced it. A silence fell about the room and a gust of wind blustered down the chimney. We both listened as the wind wailed and rattled and then died away before she spoke again.

"We cannot see the wind, *yet* we can hear it, feel its breath upon our face, and a strong gust of it can knock us down can it not? The wind can move a solid object, yet it remains unseeable to an observer. Just because we can no longer see those who have departed this world, does not mean that they are not still with us."

It was I thought a profound statement.

Viola turned from the casement.

"I can tell you a horror story if you like, do you want me to?"

I never replied because I felt that an answer was unnecessary, for I could tell she had made up her mind regardless.

"Papa, he knows all about it; you see it was his grandfather, my great-grandfather who built Star Lake Hall. Back then there was a pestilence, a scourge of the whole of Norfolk and beyond. The whole house fell sick, including most of the servants. Those who were not affected fled to the south of the country, including my great-grand-father. Apparently, he left Star Lake to escape death himself leaving his only daughter alone to care for her dying family. She was a mere child. When he returned nothing but the dead greeted him. He had all their bodies interred in the grounds of the chapel; I can show you the graves if you like!"

"How do you know all this?" I asked her.

"My grandfather told me the story when I was a little girl. He said his father told *him* the story; it seems he was full of remorse just before he died of a bad heart. You see he continued to live at Star Lake afterwards and he re-married and started a new family from which we are all now descended. There, a horror story if there ever was one," she finished.

It was indeed a shocking story and such a cold-hearted thing to do; to abandon your own family, and your only child. To let them die and then, like sweeping dust under a carpet, to simply begin again as though nothing had happened. I told Viola that I felt houses like Star Lake are like vast repositories of great memories throughout the years and often give off a sense of those memories locked away inside, in ways that can be felt such as a dark ambiance and can be experienced by anyone sensitive to such feelings. I could see she understood my meaning. What I did not add were my thoughts that sometimes these atmospheres may manifest as dreams. I now wondered if I had finally discovered the origin of my own dream of Star Lake Hall.

***

It was seven-of-the clock, and the sun was still strong on the lawns. I watched the long shadows of the trees as they stretched across the turf reaching for the house. I was now in my party gown and almost ready for the ball and was sitting at a vanity table near the window whilst Kitty fashioned my hair. The butterflies were fluttering in my stomach at the very prospect of having to meet and greet so many strangers. At the same time as feeling nervous I was happy and eager to see both my parents, so excited that I simply could not wait any longer; the prospect that they may already be in the house below was too irresistible.

I could see that Kitty was enthralled in attempting to create a work of art with my coiffure but a final glance in the looking glass told me it was finished, and I stopped Kitty from any further final improvements.

"I think that will do, and you have done a splendid job Kitty; I feel I am able to be put on show without feeling too self-conscious."

"You look lovely m'lady, you do," she said happily.

"Thank-you Kitty, I just hope I don't make a fool of myself; this gown is so long I fear I might trip over!"

"Oh no, you will be fine, I'm sure dat Mr Darlington will be ever so proud."

Kitty then placed a flower into my hair as a finishing touch, and I asked her to help fasten the glittering necklet, my birthday gift from Claude. I stood and looked at myself within the pier glass in the corner. The gown was indeed very handsome, fashioned in blue silk and properly trimmed in lace with tulle flowers.

"There, how do I look?" I asked.

"Like a princess. Oh, I wish dat I could look so fine in such a dress."

As Kitty spoke her face was alive with a blissful pleasure yet for some reason, I could sense that there was angst hidden beneath that happy veneer.

"Kitty, I hope you do not mind me asking but is there anything wrong? Anything troubling you? Is it Viola?"

I watched as she fought to keep her smile.

"Oh, it's not'eng, please don't worry about me m'lady, you go and have a lovely time at the party."

"I want you to know that you can talk to me Kitty, as friends do."

"Thank you. You are very kind but it's not'eng. Not'eng I want you to worry about tonight. Ask me again, anoder day."

"Well alright but I am always here for you Kitty, just remember that."

"I will m'lady, now go on and 'ave some fun!"

The guests were beginning to arrive and were for the most part friends and acquaintances of the family, the well-to-do, estate owners and several intellectual types. Amidst the orderly bustle I found Claude and he complimented me on my appearance and I did the same to him because he looked very handsome in his black dress coat and trousers, white waistcoat and shirt delicately plaited with small silver studs. Together we entered a Champagne refreshment room where tables were laid out with sandwiches, jellies, ices, bonbons, tea and coffee, and there was a splendid birthday cake as a centrepiece. There was a separate table where guests were leaving gifts, and the whole room was light and gay.

I saw my parents enter and hurried over to greet them. They were both as thrilled as I with the reunion and had beaming faces and my father told me how lovely I looked. My eyes welled with happy tears because I had missed them so very much. Their smiles took all their wrinkles away and the most beautiful thing about seeing my parents smile was knowing that I was the cause and reason for it. I could see in them my happy childhood, and in me they could see the future. They greeted Claude with matching affection and Henry and Dorothea came to join us.

There was much conversing, and the Hall was filled with the sound of it. I was introduced to many of Claude's friends and during the meetings I was sadly parted from my parents; however, they were being adequately cared for by Dorothea and Henry, who with my mother and father had formed an unbreakable quartet. A hired floor manager suddenly bellowed the order for the orchestra to commence and then there followed a promenade into the ballroom where all the men escorted the ladies to their seats. Everyone now had printed programmes for the evening and the introductions between guests continued and names were added to cards for the dances.

The first dance of the night I had with Claude; it was a waltz. He leaned in to kiss me.

"Will you do me the honour of dancing with me?" he said playfully, and my heart fluttered as his hand grasped mine and we began rotating and whirling.

The music was relaxed and leisurely; our feet brushed the floor as we made circles upon the marble. As I spun in the arms of my love, I saw flashes of red that only melded into Viola once the current music died. I was able to see her, an embodiment of sullenness wrapped in scarlet as she sat alone at the fringes of the ballroom.

There was a break in the music, and it was time for an exchange of dancing partners. I had danced with two of Claude's friends before a third presented himself to me. He was younger than Claude quite tall, blond, and handsome in a fresh-faced way. I was perspiring and in need of an interval. I then had a thought and asked him if he would consider dancing with Viola. I pointed to indicate where she had been sitting but now there was only a vacant seat.

"Well, I can't very well dance with a *ghost*, can I?" he said wittily, as the music began again and before I knew it, he had grabbed my hand firmly as the orchestra now began to play a livelier galoppade. As we danced my attention was constantly taken with the whereabouts of Viola. I wondered where she had gone, and I searched the room with each twirl and between each parting of hands. I hoped that I would find her among the dancers, but I could not see her.

Growing ever hotter as I continued to dance, I now began to see the little flashes of lights and the smudges of shadow that had bothered me throughout the day. These *auras* for the most part being restricted to the ends or corners of the room, the spaces devoid of partiers. At first, I put it down to the heat of the evening as it had become quite humid once the winds had died down and I was prone under such conditions to feel lightheaded after rigorous exercise.

With my eyes I tried to follow the swirling shapes as they appeared to flicker about the boundaries of the ballroom. I began to lose concentration on the dancing and the harmonisation with my partner suffered for it. My dress was getting in the way of my feet, and I became inept, standing on my partner's toes and I almost toppled and was glad when the music finally ended. Feeling embarrassed I apologised for my clumsiness and used a fan to cool myself as I left the floor.

During the respite from the dancing, I saw what I perceived to be a *form*, small in stature and unclear as one would be if veiled by a fog. This eclipsed shape in bodily form appeared to be watching me and as hard as I tried from the distance across the room, it was not easy to discern many features as the shadow remained out-of-focus to me. Whenever I glanced at it, it would scurry away to melt into the glooms, to rest beyond a crack in a doorway or a space under a table but always with the trimmings of garments left exposed. From all its hiding places I felt that it was watching me with the anxious curiosity of a child. Against the dreads that the situation was slowly creating, I walked in a direct line over to where the form now hid, shoehorned into a redundant space near a cloakroom.

As I drew near, the shape sprung from its hiding place and *swanned* across the floor and down a passageway leading to the grand entrance hall. Although gripped by feelings of foreboding I followed but could not see clearly what I was pursuing. The light was dimming as outside the sun had now sunk below the horizon and the black tide of darkness was ebbing ever closer. Climbing the grand staircases and still in pursuit of the shadow, I followed it along the balcony and up to the next floor where it suddenly faded from view. It was gone leaving me quite alone.

It was dark in the passage, there were no lamps lit and I could hear the music from the ballroom only now it sounded distorted, faint and echoey. There was almost a new sound now draped upon the orchestra. The piano and the violins had been replaced by the brittle, plucked sound of a harpsichord. The music became melancholy, old songs; Christian songs long forgotten and out of fashion. Directly before me I could now see a door and there was a flickering from under it, like the warm light cast from a snug fire. I wondered why, or who, would light a fire in August during the present sultry temperatures that a late summer always brings. I noticed that next to the door was a small painting, oil on canvass depicting a night scene of the hall, where a full moon's light silvered the rooftops. There was something about the painting that was almost entrancing, but I averted my gaze from it and knocked lightly upon the door before turning the handle.

The room beyond the door was indistinct and I could not make out much of what was inside. It was as though I was seeing into the room through a heavy veil, yet the more I concentrated and the more I sought to see, the room began to open itself to me. It was a grey room filled with the dusk's blue light. There was a fire in the grate, but the room was as cold as a spare, disused room would be. There were candles positioned upon shelves and furniture and they winked with a weak iridescence but cast hardly enough light to cut through the gloom. The firelight revealed worm-eaten panelled walls and planked floor. There were garlands of greenery fashioned from holly and ivy and they adorned the chimney piece and were strung from a central chandelier only to trail away and to disappear into the dark unseen corners of the room.

There was a more serious part about the place that impressed upon me now. All my senses told me that there were presences in the room other than my own. The longer I stood within that space the outlines of shapes, of people began to appear. I could now see the hint of forms seated upon chairs, and around small tables, and there was one who stood with his back to the room facing the single casement, looking out into the moonless night beyond. I had the feeling that the longer I remained in the room the more a part of it I would become. I could now almost feel the trace of warmth from the fire's insipid flames. I even began to smell the burning wax from the guttering candles placed here and there. I started doubting that I was experiencing these things and that the whole room was merely a symptom of nervous dyspepsia!

Feeling fearful, I backed away from the fire and the frozen silhouettes of people and turned to leave the room, but I could no longer see the door; there existed now only a wall of shadow. Frantically, I felt about for a doorhandle but as my hands met with the shadows, they almost became part of them, becoming inky remnants of my own flesh.

The door has to be here, I told myself over and over and I closed my eyes and pictured the door-frame where it had been, and then my hand found the cold brass handle.

The air in the room became thinner; it was so hard for me to breathe. I turned one final time to look into the room and saw how the shapes, the silhouettes were gaining substance; the fire had now developed a definite *crack* as tiny sparks burst from the tinder dry logs within. I began to see the faces of those forms seated around a small card table, merely impressions as though daubed in limpid colours using a pallet of greys and whites and the dimmest of blue. I could still hear the music played upon a harpsichord with such despondency from below and I thought about the party and my parents and Claude, and I wanted to leave this fusty, unfavourable place and join them downstairs.

Rushing outside, I pulled the door shut behind me. My breathing was laboured, my legs wobbly, and my head felt light. Then I saw her coming down the passage towards me. A white mask topping a cerise gown, the only colour in our darkened space. I was looking into the eyes of the papier-mâché face that I had seen earlier in Viola's room. There was a sensation that the floor was moving from under me and the whole scene was rapidly being wiped to fog by my own infirmity. Moments before I met with the floor I realised where I had seen that ashen face with the fractured skin before. It was one of the faces from my dream, a face held frozen within the crystalline snow.

I woke in my bed to find an elderly gentleman at my side; he was holding my wrist and staring at his fob watch. The drapes were drawn, and a lamp was burning on top of a chiffonier and his own wizened face shone like a lantern under the lamplight. It was still late evening and I assumed rightly that the man with his fingertips gently resting on my pulse was a doctor. By his manner of dress, I assumed he had been a guest at the party. When I turned my head, I could see Claude and my parents and Henry and Dorothea, and all wore such worried expressions.

"Tell me my dear, how are you feeling? You might be experiencing a little confusion now that you have regained consciousness," said the doctor.

"I feel quite alright, just a little tired. What happened?"

For the moment I remembered nothing, only that I had been dancing and feeling hot and a little lightheaded.

"You have nothing to worry about, you just suffered a little syncopal episode, nothing more. It is quite common for one in your present condition."

"My condition?" I replied, not quite understanding the doctor's comment. Then I saw the look on my mother's face, and upon Dorothea's and I guessed rightly the reason for my black out before the doctor spoke again.

"I am happy to announce that you are with child!"

Before I could react, Claude was at my side and the doctor and the rest of the family were congratulating us.

"Are-are you certain?" I asked.

A smile spread across the doctor's benevolent face.

"Oh, quite sure my dear, I have been a practicing physician for a considerable time, and I am never wrong about these things!"

The news that had just been delivered, although unexpected, did seem right. Somehow, I knew. The little twinges, the slight queasiness when waking. I was thrilled and scared, and a multitude of different emotions overwhelmed me in a trice.

"For the second time in my life, you my darling Bella have made me the happiest man alive," said Claude, and he kissed me lightly on my forehead.

It then all came flooding back to me, the discovery of the room and the uncanny ghostlike forms within. I let out a sudden gasp when I remembered the white features of the mask as I must have slumped to the floor.

"What is it that troubles you?" Claude said, with growing alarm at my facial expression, which no doubt was filled with angst.

It was Dorothea who spoke next.

"Do not worry my dear, I know how it feels, the shock of knowing you have a new life growing inside you. You have nothing to fear, we as your family will look after you. You have made us all so very happy!"

I then simply thanked Dorothea, and everybody, and my dearest parents came again to embrace me and to pass on all their good blessings. For a moment I even thought that the whole affair of that strange room had been something that I had dreamt whilst lying in this very bed. I wished that it had only been that, a dream but some wishes are never granted.

***

During the following day it felt as though I had been gaoled to my bedchamber as Claude insisted that I remained in bed for the whole day after the ball. I know he was only concerned for my well-being and now for that of our child. I still have not got used to those thoughts, *our child*. My child. Kitty was delighted with the news as I thought she would be. She had heard a rumour about the house, but I confirmed it for her when she brought my breakfast tray. I asked her to stay a while as I needed to talk to another woman about the things that were worrying me.

"Oh, I wonder what sort of mother I will be, a good one I hope," I said, restively. Kitty sat on the edge of my bed and smiled.

"You will be a fine mum m'lady, you are nurturing, tough, fun, and protective of those you care for, and if you are afraid m'lady den it can only mean you will be fine as a mum because you realise 'aving a child is 'aving a new living soul to be responsible for. I 'ave no doubt, dat you'll be a natural." Kitty truly was a godsend right now and I thanked her for her enriching words, and it showed me just how much our lives differed for those words to have come from someone as young as she.

I had learned from Claude that it was Viola who had discovered me lying in the passage on the night of the party. She had notified Baxter, as bell cords were not installed in that particular part of the house, and Baxter had then carried me to my room. When I met with Viola one morning in the drawing room, I thanked her for her favour, and I bestowed upon her a small gift of a fine set of art brushes that she could use for her papier-mâché creations, but her thanks were on the whole perfunctory. She asked me what I had been doing in that old wing of the house as the family seldom frequent it on account of the 'atmosphere'. I spun her a tale of my condition bringing upon me a fever resulting in confusion and finding myself lost within the house. I had no intention of bringing up the matter of the *room* with her or even with Claude, at least not until I had made sense of it myself. I did wonder why Viola herself was present, wandering the passages but I never asked, and I imagined she had simply grown bored of the party and sought some solitude in the only available places the house offered.

One day during luncheon-time the whole family remained indoors due to a light rain that had remained persistent since the morning. Claude's happiness at the prospect of becoming a father was a joy to see. He was already talking about how his son or daughter would be taught all that he knew of the heavens above us. He even began to discuss naming the child with the rest of the family. I had not thought about what name to give our child, but Claude seemed adamant that if the child were a boy, he should be named after his great-grandfather Richard Augustus Darlington who built Star Lake Hall.

I was not very content regarding this choice only because of the story Viola had divulged, in fact, she looked at me artfully when Claude mentioned it in order to see my reaction. I could never name my son, if we were to have a son, after such a hard-hearted man as Richard Darlington. That cold man who abandoned his own family leaving them to face pestilential death without so much as an afterthought to their welfare. Following Claude's suggestion, I came to believe that perhaps he did not know the story that Viola knew because if he did, he would not have suggested such a thing. I don't know why, it might be called a *mother's intuition,* but I somehow felt that the life growing inside me could well be a girl, and if so, I would call her Amelia after my mother.

It was late in the afternoon and not quite dinnertime. I issued from the house for my daily turn around the gardens. The light rain had given out to a warm breeze that tugged at my parasol and rippled the grass creating steady waves. I sat for a while amongst the tufts and enjoyed the delightful chirruping of birds as they hopped from twig to branch, warmed by the sun's golden rays. As ever the gardens were overshadowed by the enormity of the house and I gazed up at it, at all the windows and chimney stacks and my mind turned back to the night I had entered that puzzling room. I was sure that some of my memories of it had been coloured by what had been my impendent blackout. Over the course of the ensuing days, I had even begun to doubt the room's existence at all. To put my mind at rest I decided that before dinner I would retrace my steps the best that I could remember and go to look for the room.

I wandered the upper passages of Star Lake Hall but kept out of sight and merged with the glooms when I saw Mrs Dexter and Baxter both discussing the condition of this part of the house. Mrs Dexter was fussing over the shabby floor coverings that had become worn in places; Baxter seemed more interested in the cracks in the plasterwork and I overheard him mentioning the possibility of structural problems for the house. I remained in my hidey-hole until both had passed by and turned the corner. Finding myself finally alone I proceeded along the passage and stopped where I felt the room ought to have been, yet there was only a flat wall, and it was void of any door at all.

I was certain that I was in the same place, as confident as I could be, given the circumstances of my weakness that night. I walked up and along adjoining passages but they were furnished with articles, and display cabinets all filled with preserved birdlife that I did not recall seeing on the night of the party. I came back to the spot where I was sure I must have fainted. It was a definite conclusion that there was no door, but my instincts had not failed me because I saw the little painting of the house in the moonlight and then I knew I was at the right place.

I could not explain the fact that the door was no longer there; it was after all incomprehensible that an entire room could simply cease to exist. I now unhooked the small painting and I scrutinised it and saw that there was a title and a name brushed with delicacy at the bottom right corner, it read: 'House of shadows LD'. As I stood in the passage, I came to understand Viola's words when she mentioned that the family seldom visited this part of the house due to the 'atmosphere'. This area of the house was steeped in shadow and silence, and it made me feel quite uneasy. Clutching the painting I left the passage taking the long route for my own atelier where I placed the painting upon the easel. I read the description again and then realised that the initials LD must surely denote that the artist was *Laurence Darlington*. I covered the painting when I heard Kitty's light knocks on my door; it was time to get ready for dinner.

Chapter VI
Holly Lane House

Summertime had taken its last bow and slipped from the stage to make space for the next act. Autumn had quickly filled the vacancy and summer was now again in temporary repose. The grounds about the hall had become enriched with seasonal blooms of red and gold, almost as though to soothe summertime's slumber until she was ready to rise again and indulge us, mere mortals in her genuine golden warmth. As I sat near a window in the morning room I watched as a groundsman swept the fallen leaves and twigs and then carted them over to a bonfire which he had built upon the wasteland near to the old summerhouse; the slight breeze pushing its odour towards the house.

During the last few days Claude had gradually slipped back into his observatory and would do so with regularity most evenings and early mornings. He carries a passion for his science and I cannot hold that against him, but I do wish he would visit his turret less often. I have experienced no further preternatural occurrences such as the flitting shadows or the emergence of ethereal doorways to equally mystifying rooms. These, in part had once come to me during moments of solitude. I confess that since the family learned of my *condition*, I have found myself meticulously coddled by Dorothea, Claude, and Henry. Being of lighter weight with a small midsection I had started to show, as my stomach had formed a little pregnant bulge. I was made to sit down and to take every sort of precaution possible. It was becoming tedious, and I so missed my regular walks outside without a chaperone at hand.

One afternoon when Claude was in his observatory and I was, as had been the standard, quite unemployed, I decided to go and find Henry so that I could request a coach to take me to visit my parents. I do not know why I had not thought of it sooner, as the change of scenery would do me the world of good and I was sure Claude would be of the same opinion and perhaps would ask to accompany me.

I knocked lightly upon Henry's study door and the door being unlocked swung open. There was nobody inside and I was about to leave to go and see if I could find him elsewhere when my eyes caught sight of a full-length portrait that hung on a wall behind his desk. The portrait was rather striking and being artistically inclined I wanted to know who was presented in the picture. I walked inside the room and stood within reach of the painting. There was a little brass inscription plate on the bottom of the gilded frame - it read: *Richard Augustus Darlington*. I stood back to take in the large portrait of the man who had built Star Lake Hall, the man who had allegedly abandoned his family whilst they had perished from an infection.

Richard Darlington looked to be tall and slender, and he had been painted in a relaxed yet dynamic pose. The portrait had an exquisitely painted face and hands, and the overall expression of the subject was one of intellect. Richard was depicted as youthful; a young and impatient man eager to obtain all the riches that life had to offer and a resoluteness shone from his unyielding blue stare that said nothing would be allowed to stand in his way of achieving it. He had been portrayed as almost regal in lavish, richly coloured robes. Richard Augustus Darlington nearly loomed outward from the canvas because of the absence of any bright landscaped background.

Turning from the portrait I saw the little red poetry book that had once belonged to Laurence was resting upon a small lamp table. I picked it up for I was sure that Henry would not mind if I borrowed it again. Clutching the book, I left the study and hid myself away in the conservatory adjoining the library. Before seating myself amongst the potted houseplants, I selected a large volume from one of the library shelves: the subject was irrelevant as I only wanted to use it to conceal the book of poems so that I could study it unnoticed by others. I was sure the book held more answers regarding the mysterious room.

Towards the back of the book, I discovered some scribbled wording as footnotes. Someone, and I can only assume it was Laurence, had written:

'It keeps itself locked away from me, out of reach until it wants me to find it!'

I knew at once the meaning of these words. Laurence had discovered the room. What Henry said about his brother was beginning to make sense. Henry had talked about Laurence becoming obsessed with something in the house. He had mentioned his brother 'scrutinising old plans of the house', and then there was Henry's almost cautionary request that I should promise:

'Not to go poking around the house, exploring, looking for secret doors to secret rooms that frankly do not exist'.

I felt at once that Laurence's disappearance and the mysterious room were connected. Had he wandered into the room to become somehow ensnared within it? I remembered the shadows of the *others* I had perceived whilst inside the room myself. I remembered the one whose back was turned to the room as he stood facing the casement window. Was this the same figure I had seen from outside the house? Had this become Laurence's fate?

The very legends about the house spoken by Kitty, alluded to it being a silent accomplice to the periodic disappearances of those who dwelt within. The house I felt would not betray its secrets lightly, and now confronted by its muteness, I felt powerless to be able to break its shyness by any *earthly* means. I would have to wait for whatever reason it needed in order to open itself to me again, but would I possess the courage to look further a second time? Should I?

I then discovered within the book another message to test my promptitude of thought on the matter. In a heavier hand and almost *carved* into the page were the simple words:

'Her gift to me'.

He had attempted to illustrate the meaning of his words for he had sketched what looked like a baby – no, a doll. His depiction of the doll was so skilfully produced that I was in no doubt that it was the same doll I had first seen left upon the grass by the old summerhouse, then later wrapped as a birthday offering to me. I was also now sure that Laurence *was* the artist who had painted the picture of Star Lake under moonlight that presently rested upon my easel.

***

It was a bright morning and I had managed for once to slip outside unnoticed and without a *shepherd* at my elbow. I had no sooner walked across the terrace amongst the chairs that were now neatly stacked and covered for the looming winter months when I heard a voice. I recognised it as Viola's, and she was scolding someone in her usual condescending and haughty manner. As I came around the rotunda of the outdoor kitchen, I saw Kitty on her knees and in tears scrubbing the stone paving with Viola presiding over her as she worked.

As I approached, Viola was surprised to see me, and she quickly dismissed Kitty who scurried away still weeping as she slipped into a door at the back of the house. Feeling nettled by what I had seen I demanded an explanation from Viola, who was forthright with her reply.

"The flagging here is discoloured by moss and dirt I asked the Irish girl to remove it! I find it unpleasant when looking down from my bedchamber window," she said.

"Surely that is a job for one of the groundsmen?" I declared, and I confess that the whole affair had ruffled me to the point where I was quite riled.

"Why should I go and bother the men whom I expect have enough important and more pressing work to do when I find Kitty, your Irish maid, being true to her indolent ways and dozing in the kitchen garden!"

"Nevertheless, Kitty attends to me and me alone, and I hope this settles the matter. I need a maid able to help me in my present condition and not one who is exhausted because of the strenuous chores that *you* have given her."

Viola crossed her arms and marched away with her nose in the air leaving me with a pounding heart as I watched her re-enter the house.

I decided to go and find Kitty to see if she was all right. I found her in her own quarters below the main house and she was still visibly upset. I told her that I had had words with Viola, and this worried Kitty, but I assured her that there would be no further bother from my sister-in-law as I had been quite clear and firm on the matter. This did not seem to lighten Kitty's anxiety, and she admitted being found asleep by Viola when she should have been working.

"I am so sorry m'lady, but I 'ave had a lot of trouble sleeping at night," she explained. I asked her why this was so.

"Oh, sweet mother of Jaysus! I 'ave tried to keep it all to myself, I never wanted to say anyt'eng about it!"

"About what Kitty? What has been troubling you?"

Kitty's eyes appeared fear-haunted in her ashen face.

"Oh, it's the spirits of dis place m'lady, rattling me door, knocking on de walls, it's put me mind crossways it has, I'm scared to death!"

I was shocked to hear what Kitty said, as I was

now aware that the house had a *presence* but so far to me at least, it seemed to be reticent. What Kitty now said implied that it had developed a malign quality.

"Kitty, are you sure you did not imagine all this? Sometimes the wind it can—"

"Parden me m'lady but I didn't come down in de last shower! I know what I 'eard, what I saw. I saw me doorknob rattle with me own eyes as if someone 'ad a grip of it, and de knocking, de calling!"

"Calling?"

"It was calling me name m'lady, calling *me*. It's got me nerves up. I'm so scared!"

I took up Kitty's hand and tried my best to sooth her until she was calm. I then told her that I was planning a trip to visit my parents and wanted her to come with me.

"Oh, m'lady, do you mean dat. I'd love to come, anyt'eng to get away from this place."

"Of course I mean it, and when you come back all these troubles will have blown away."

"God luv us, I pray dat you're right."

"I am right Kitty, you will see."

"When do we go?"

"Well, as soon as it can be arranged, it might be a couple of days. Will you be all right?"

"Yes, and t'ank you m'lady, you are very kind. I just need to keep out of Miss Viola's way."

"I told you I have spoken to her, she will not give you any more trouble, and if she does, I shall deal with it."

"It's just dat, and excuse me language, she reckons I need a kick up the arse and a map of the world! I'm not lazy m'lady, just tired."

"I know Kitty, why don't you take the rest of the morning off, have a sleep, I shall be all right and I will cover for you should anyone ask."

"T'ank you m'lady, dat would be lovely, dat's if you don't mind?"

"Not at all. You need the rest."

Kitty lay upon her bed and closed her eyes.

"If Miss Viola could see me now, she'd crack a nut. She's got a face dat would make an onion cry, and I reckon, some bad problems up the frock too!"

We both dissolved into giggles with Kitty's last remark, and it helped lighten the mood. Soon Kitty was slipping into some much-needed sleep, and I crept out of her room and quietly closed the door.

***

The arrangements for my trip to stay with my parents had been made. Claude said that he would come to join me at Holly Lane House towards the end of my stay and would then accompany me on the return journey back to Star Lake Hall. He explained that around the middle of October *Uranus*, a celestial body (the name of which was unfamiliar to me) would be at its brightest and according to Claude, is always so terribly difficult to see because of its faintness but a new moon showing black in the night sky would create the special conditions that enabled one to view it by telescope. I could see that he was excited at the prospect, and I didn't mind too much as the day prior to my trip we spent together in its entirety without any distractions to come between us.

It was a rosy dawn the morning of my departure. The excitement and anticipation of returning to Holly Lane House had wakened me early for I had missed the place immeasurably. Luggage was loaded onto the coach whilst I took breakfast with the family. Claude could hardly detach himself from my side and fussed terribly when the time came for me to depart. I left the hall as though it was a large puzzle box, with all its perplexities locked away from each and every one of us, only offering fleeting glimpses in the twilight to those with a curious leaning.

The journey to Holly Lane House would take less than an hour and during the period I talked with Kitty, describing my childhood home and assuring her how kindly and good-natured both my parents were, and that they would be most accommodating towards her as my maid. I explained that the house was not anywhere near as majestic as Star Lake Hall but nevertheless a delightful country house all the same. I explained how my parents did not have a need for a large body of domestic staff, there was only Ada our housekeeper-cook, and Oscar and Jack, head groom and stable boy. We usually did most of the work ourselves.

The coach finally took a turn down Holly Lane itself and it was only when I saw the holly trees lining the road that I truly felt I was coming home. The trees were so old now and had matured to grand old wives adorning the lane with their deep green leaves all glossy in the autumn morning sunlight. The leaves were stippled with an abundance of red berries. I recalled my grandmother once telling me how that was a sign of a deep and harsh winter to come.

'Those old trees know what is coming, and all the birds need feeding throughout the winter,' she would say.

I have since learnt from Henry however, that a vibrant rash of berry upon a tree has more to do with the seasons past than those to come. Apparently, a tree needs only a warm summer to make berries.

The reunion with my parents was wonderful and in no time at all, with Kitty's help, I was unpacked and settled in my old room that during my absence from Holly Lane had been kept clean but unaltered. Kitty was indeed welcomed and was shown to her room by Ada the housekeeper and I could see how happy the change had made her as it had made me.

The days at Holly Lane passed too quickly and due to my condition, I endured the same level of cossetting as I had when at Star Lake. One chilly afternoon the wind had whipped up and had shaken the sycamores bare to now stand naked amongst the hollies that curtained the house. During the evening we ate a scrumptious roast dinner prepared by Ada and Kitty and I made sure that each had a plateful too. The first fire of the autumn was lit, and we sat near to it and the smell of the burning cherry wood was delightful. My father called Ada and asked her to prepare some drinking chocolate. I talked of my new life at Star Lake and about Claude and his observatory and his passion for charting everything that moved in the heavens.

"Oh, Bella it sounds like a darling old house," said my mother, and I so wanted to share her feelings about my new home but that longstanding wandering place had presented another side unto me and anyone else who cared to look too deeply. I then mentioned Claude's late uncle Laurence, and surprisingly my father then shared some memories about a commotion that had sprung out from Star Lake estate back in the day.

"I remember a search party of men from the Hall coming to the village looking for the gentleman you speak of," said my father. "At the time it looked as though the old Darlington ghosts had taken another," he chuckled as he used an iron to stir the fire.

"So, you knew the stories Father?"

I was astonished that having known about the strange accounts, neither of my parents had ever mentioned it before.

"Oh yes Bella, it was always common talk amongst the townsfolk far and wide."

"What do they say?" I asked, and as we talked, I was unaware that Kitty had entered the room carrying a tray lined with a chocolate pot and cups and saucers.

"Only the old tale about the Darlington ghost snatching people, where the poor unfortunates are never to be seen again. All nonsense of course …"

My father was silenced when Kitty dropped the salver she carried in fright of what he had said. She staggered amid the broken crockery and pooling chocolate with hands to her chest as she tried desperately to control her fear.

"For goodness' sake, pray, sit down child," my father bade, and she collapsed in a heap into the nearest armchair. My parents both looked to me for an explanation.

"I'm afraid Kitty finds the Hall a worrisome place, she is … sensitive to the atmospheres within it, and to stories like the one you have spoken of Father."

"My dear child, you do not mean you believe in all that tommyrot, do you?" he said astonished.

"I do Sir, yes I do believe it. 'Tis why I 'ave come

with m'lady to 'ave some time free of it."

Kitty then looked at me with excusatory eyes.

"I am so sorry m'lady, for de mess I've made. I will clean it up, I'm not usually so clumsy."

Kitty paid no attention to my subsequent reassurances, she quickly collected up all the broken china and hurried away to fetch a cloth.

I checked on Kitty before I retired for bed and was happy to see that she was now quite unruffled although she remained apologetic over the damage to my parent's chocolate set. The wind was still strong outside and gusted against the glass and down the chimney as I lay in bed. I had lit a lamp and picked up Laurence's poetry book that had rested upon the bedside table. I could not find any further enigmatic messages, footnotes, or sketches and I found it odd that he would use this book as a diary of sorts. I turned down the wick on the lamp and pushed all thoughts about the incongruousness of Star Lake to the back of my mind, or so I thought.

Chapter VII
The unveiling

It was just like the painting. The moonlight shining over the house. The snow-capped roof luminous under the moon's frosty light. I was standing before Star Lake Hall holding a lantern. I knew I was in the dream again. I always know but this time it was different.

I followed the tracks and soon I could see the circle of trees but here they were not lifeless and brittle, only sleeping and clothed in whiteness.

This time I had no desire to enter the doors and to wander the ice-encrusted labyrinth within, to see the faces of woe staring up through the ice with their doom ridden eyes. I had seen it all countless times before.

I turned my back on the house and I walked away into the night, across the snow-white brilliance, holding my lantern before me; it was the softest of light. I was making deep footprints across the unblemished snow and then under the candlelight I saw another's trail and the imprints were smaller, as if made by a child's foot. I followed the tracks and soon I could see the circle of trees but here they were not lifeless and brittle, only sleeping and clothed in whiteness. Within their midst I saw the summerhouse, not decrepit and ramshackle as I know it to be but new and standing strong and covered in flawless white.

The footprints led up to the summerhouse and as I came close, I could hear a sobbing, like that of a child weeping softly in a forsaken manner. Gingerly, I stepped into the darkness, the core of the summerhouse. The fire in my lantern now burned weakly and it reminded me of the candles I had seen in the *mysterious room* and how they barely managed to produce their feeble light. The sobbing continued and then there came that skin prickling moment as I realised that the shadow cast by the lamplight was not my own.

I stopped moving and I watched the shadow sat upon the floor as it cradled something in its dusky arms. I looked harder at the bone white article, and I saw it was a doll, *the doll;* the doll I had unwrapped from its paper and vine and then watched as it had been cast into the lifeless fire grate and then viciously smashed and gored with a fire iron. The form sobbed and wept as though its vaporous soul could wring a river from its dim eyes due to the enormity of the sorrow it suffered. The dark form upon the floor seemed to be mending the doll, dabbing each sliver of china about its eyes, as though its tears provided the glue required to bond the pieces together.

I was afraid but I had a desire to speak out to the shadow on the floor; I felt a need to give it some form of comfort as the weeping continued miserably.

"I am sorry about the doll, I never meant for it to be broken," I said, and all at once the sobbing ceased and the child turned to me and then I saw her fully as the snow outside reflected upon her already chilled soul. The child was a wraith in tattered rags, and she had the face akin to a china doll whose skin was a lattice of faults and splits, with deep-set eyes and teeth displayed in an unpleasant fiendish grin. With an unearthly pace she grabbed for me.

I woke in my darkened room and in my haste

to turn up the wick on my lamp I almost knocked it from the bedside table. With my room now bathed in a protective shell of light, I propped myself with pillows and tried to distance myself from the dream which had after so many years finally made the leap into the realms of true nightmares. The unyielding blustery weather outside did not help to calm my nerves and I wished that Claude was here beside me and not a long way off at Star Lake and probably in that turret of his. Then in an instant I knew what I needed to do.

I climbed out of bed and removed the drapes from the casement window. There was no moon. The sky was dark and naked from cloud and the stars could be seen to glimmer within it. I searched for the paired stars that Claude had shown me that night before we made love and fell asleep beneath them. After a little searching, I spotted them and remembered Claude's words:

'You see the stars Bella, that is us and whenever you look up there, we shall be, you and I side by side in perpetuity.'

I returned to my bed keeping the stars in sight and when I was able to lower the wick once more, there they were, and it was a great comfort and in no time at all I had drifted towards peaceful sleep.

***

It was my last day at Holly Lane House. The

morning was bright as the clouds had been wiped from the sky by the raging winds the previous night and replaced by stillness. When I saw Kitty in my room she apologised for her clumsiness and again I told her that it was nothing for her to worry over.

"It was de shock of 'earing what your dad said," explained Kitty, and she then spoke of a face she had seen peering over her when she was in bed, the night before we both came to Holly Lane. I asked her to describe the face.

"It was 'orrible m'lady, all white and broken; I screamed and buried myself under de blankets. When I was brave enough to look again, whatever it was 'ad gone. I don't want to go back to Star Lake m'lady, I'm too afraid!"

Kitty's hands were shaking, and I knew then I couldn't take her back with me today so I told her that I would ask if she could stay here with my parents for a little while, and I would tell Mrs Dexter that she had suffered a fever and needed to recover at Holly Lane. I was sure old Ada could do with the extra help; I had noticed that she had been walking around much more slowly and stiffly as though her joints were causing her pain.

"I would love to stay 'ere m'lady, I truly would but I couldn't leave you now dat you're expecting."

"It's early days Kitty, I will be fine and adequately cared for back at Star Lake. Let me do this for you and I will send for you when I need you, and when your nerves are stronger."

"If you are sure m'lady?"

"I am sure. I will arrange it before breakfast."

"T'ank you m'lady, you are so very kind."

I was able to convince my parents that Kitty would be no burden upon them and a great help now that I was no longer living at Holly Lane. It took a little persuasion, only due to Kitty's behaviour the previous night. Kitty had helped Ada to serve us breakfast and I could see from her flushed, usually ashen face that she still carried with her the burden of embarrassment. During the clearing away of the breakfast things, my father waited for Ada and Kitty to leave the room before he spoke.

"That maid of yours, she is a nice enough girl but is she completely sane? All this believing in ghosts! I can assure her that after surviving thrice the sum of birthdays as she has had, the only spirits I have ever seen are those racked up behind bartenders my dear," he jocosely insisted.

"Like I have already mentioned, Kitty has a sensitive nature and Star Lake is such a rambling old place. It is I believe a lot easier to dismiss ghosts in the daylight," I said, thinking of my own experiences that up till now I had kept to myself. It was then my mother who surprised us both with her feelings on the subject.

"Perhaps Kitty is right to be frightened, after all, the dead do far outnumber the living," she said. My father was somewhat shocked by my mother's apparent support for the acceptance of ghosts. Before he could add anything more on the subject, we all fell silent as we listened to the sound of a coach approaching the house.

"That must be Claude," I announced and quickly got to my feet and went over to the windows where I could see that it was indeed one of Star Lake's coaches with Watson driving. When the coach stopped its door sprung open, and Claude jumped down onto the path. I hurried to get outside to greet him.

I had missed Claude and he was pleased to see me as I had hoped he would be. He had arrived without an attendant, and I noticed how tired his eyes were; leaden clouds had gathered around them, and he appeared fagged almost to the very margin of illness. He dismissed his appearance as the product of a series of late nights in his observatory but seemed sprightly and cheerful enough. The morning was spent in the company of my parents and Claude talked with my father almost endlessly about his passion for starwatching.

My final day at Holly Lane was racing by and I willed the clocks to stop, yet their pointers continued to circle the face with what seemed to be an ever-increasing pace. Soon we were having dinner and the coach was being loaded with my luggage by Watson who had remained at Holly Lane since Claude's arrival. After dinner I spoke with Claude and explained the situation with Kitty. He was very understanding of her troubles and full of empathy and I knew then just what kind of a father he would be.

As always it was a sad separation as I said my goodbyes and left my parents at Holly Lane House. It was dark as the coach left and the moonlight shone upon the glistening leaves of the old holly trees and the trills of night birds were carried on a freshly roused breeze. We fastened the windows on the coach, and both sat snug inside. Claude then took up my hand and he turned to me in a manner that told me he had something to tell me that I might find troubling.

"Darling Bella, there is something I need to share with you. I know you sometimes find it difficult to understand the passion I have for the worlds that drift across the heavens and for the stars that act as beacons within that vast expanse above," he said, with worry in his voice.

"Whatever is bothering you my love, pray let it be told. Tell me Claude."

"Very well. You see there is to be a transit of Venus across the face of the sun. The previous time this happened was in 1769, over a century ago! The precise timing measurements of the passage of Venus across the Sun, made from different locations around the globe, can be used to determine the precise distance of our world from the

Sun."

"Well, what has this to do with you?"

"In the past, these timings and observations were a challenge to make with any accuracy. Most men who have tried were only partially successful. The astronomical society of which I am a member is planning on several expeditions around the world, including Honolulu, Thebes and Cape Town. I have been asked to accompany a very learned astronomer to Thebes, where we shall be equipped with portable telescopes and instruments to measure the transit. They are already constructing the temporary observation huts. If we succeed in successful measurements, it could be the making of my whole career."

Claude's face was alight with enthusiasm; I could see he had been offered the kind of opportunity that if not taken, would over time turn into a heavy chain of regret for him to carry about his person. I had no idea of the place of which he spoke, it sounded so distant, so exotic.

"The place you speak of, Thebes, where in the world is it?"

"It lies within central Greece."

"How long would you be away?"

"Not very long my love, and fortunately I will return in plenty of time for the event that I am constantly bursting with joy in anticipation of," he said, as he placed a hand upon my stomach. "However Bella, if my absence would cause you trouble or worry then I will *not* go. You have my word on that."

As he spoke, I could see the shadow of disappointment fall across his face. I fell in love with him because of his youthful enthusiasm for the world and now it seems, other worlds. I did not want him to put to rest all the dreams and ambitions he held so dear just so that he could become a husband and a father; to grow old without his passion for the world and its possibilities. I know that men do not turn their backs on dreams because they grow old; they grow old *because* they stop dreaming.

"I would never ask you not to go. I know how much this means to you. When would you be leaving?"

"Oh Bella, I simply do not deserve your love. You have made me very happy indeed!"

He leaned in to kiss me and a bump in the road then divided us again.

"I will be leaving in early November and returning mid-to-late December at the very latest."

"So long? Does a world need so many days to travel past the sun?" I asked.

Claude chuckled, "Oh no my love but I need to set up the equipment and ensure that everything is working as it should in preparation for the event itself."

"I see. Oh, I shall miss you but you shall leave with my blessing."

"I thank you with all of my heart. My parents were not as understanding as you are my darling.

I shall work incredibly hard so that this venture will make my name in the field of astronomy; I will do it for you and our child to be."

***

Mrs Dexter sat up straight in her chair behind her desk; she bore the same stern expression that she always wore. When I explained that Kitty was too unwell to leave Holly Lane House, she listened with her eyebrow cocked and I could sense that she did not believe the falsehood I had put to her. Without anything to corroborate otherwise she had to accept my story, although she made it clear that: "She will not receive a single ha'penny from the coffers of Star Lake, and when she returns, she will have double duties for a week!"

I did not doubt Mrs Dexter's word on the matter, but I knew that Kitty would be fairly paid for her work at my parent's house, and I would ensure to keep her duties towards me as light as possible on her return until she had finally slipped from under Mrs Dexter's scrutiny. My rejection of an interim maid was accepted without any fuss as both Mrs Dexter and I knew the reality of how difficult that would be to arrange.

When I left the housekeeper's room I slipped outside because I had missed my little walks around the estate. I had not visited the family chapel since arriving at the house; it seemed such a forlorn place but the appearance of the headstones rising through the wild grass were alluring in a melancholy sort of way. This end of the park, like its opposite boundary that contained the assembly of dead trees, was somewhat untamed, wild, and windswept, and the grass was tussocky and wet with the autumn dew. I was fearful of slipping in my present state and had to watch my footing carefully as I roamed between the graves, stopping occasionally to read the inscriptions. As I looked upon the face of the headstones, I could feel each epitaph penetrating through the cool morning air almost like breaths enticing me to stop and read further. There was one marker laid flat and its surface had been tooled to create the impression of a sleeping child. There was a name upon it which read: *Esther Anne Darlington.* It was a sad little grave and I recalled the story from Viola about how Claude's great-grandfather, Richard Darlington had abandoned his family to escape a sickness that had swept over the household, and how his youngest daughter was left to care for her sick family until she succumbed to the malaise herself. Was I now standing over her grave?

The chapel itself now unused, was almost a ruin. Creepers and trees had attempted to reclaim the spot where it stood. The trees that flanked the stone structure were stout and old and their branches overshadowed it and clawed at its stone skin when pushed by the wind. The small windows still retained the colourful glass and had kept the weather out and I slipped in through the unlocked doorway. The chapel was empty save for a set of wooden pews and a raised stone font. Webbing drooped between the beams and joists and the whole space inside was gloomy as the light from outside was cut off by the overgrowth of tree and bush. It struck me then how a chapel should never simply seem gloomy, and if shadows are trapped within where they cling to corners thriving where the sunlight no longer roams, then they should serve as places of reflection, allowing the thoughts of observers to wander amongst them, to seek light, truth, and holiness.

As I peered into one such murky crook, I saw a wooden plaque fixed to the wall. It had been carved so that its top and bottom trimmings resembled a paper scroll. Upon this plaque was a register of names dating back to *1633*, a family tree. Charmed by my discovery I came close to read the list:

DOUGLAS AUGUSTUS DARLINGTON—
LUELLA FLORENCE ASTLEY. 1633
[LUELLA JANE DARLINGTON, LILY FLORENCE
DARLINGTON, JAMES HENRY DARLINGTON]

~

JAMES HENRY DARLINGTON—
CLEMENTINE CAPELL. 1693
[RICHARD AUGUSTUS DARLINGTON]

~

*RICHARD AUGUSTUS DARLINGTON
—ANNE MAY CLIFFORD. 1748
[JACOB AUGUSTUS DARLINGTON, RICHARD
HENRY DARLINGTON, ESTHER
ANNE DARLINGTON]*

~

*RICHARD AUGUSTUS DARLINGTON
—MARY LANGER. 1777
[GEORGE RICHARD DARLINGTON, JUDITH
CATHERINE DARLINGTON]*

~

*GEORGE RICHARD DARLINGTON—EVELYN
ANNE FRANKLAND. 1809
[HENRY RICHARD DARLINGTON, LAURENCE
JACOB DARLINGTON]*

I saw his name, he who had built Star Lake Hall - Richard Darlington, and there *she* was, Esther Darlington, his only daughter. It seemed the story I had heard was true after all as the list started over with a new marriage for Richard and it ended with Henry and Laurence. I felt a wrench of sadness as I saw how one family had been pitilessly erased from time, only to be replaced by another. Equally I knew that I would not be stood here if that family line had not been broken, with Claude as my husband and our child budding within me. A wind picked up and moaned as it swept around the chapel, and I heard another sound, a voice calling my name. I recognised the voice to be Claude's.

I walked back amongst the graves until I spotted Claude making his way along by the yew trees at the perimeter of the burial ground. I called to him and waved, and he stopped and waited for me to join him; he had it seemed, been looking for me.

"Why do you come here of all places?" he asked, as the wind gained more force to push against us and we rocked on our feet under a fresh gust.

"I wanted to see the chapel, why has it been left to decline so?"

"Oh, I expect that is because it is merely a relic from another time, a forgotten time. We've never used it. Not during my lifetime anyway," he said.

I was feeling cold as the wind had developed a bite. We talked as we walked back to the house about the chapel and about the plaque inscribed with the Darlington family tree. Claude, it seemed had never seen it but he knew enough about his own lineage from the collection of portraits of his ancestors that were scattered about the house, amply illuminating his own descent.

As we walked across the lawns with the frontage of the house in full view, I spotted the mystifying window, its shy presence now once again fully exposed. I saw the figure standing, rigid, motionless and I felt him watching us, watching me. It was merely a shadow at the window, but the gloom of the morning meant that the form was more pronounced and backlit from the light in the room behind it. I stopped walking and gripped Claude's arm.

"The figure in the window, can you see it?" I asked.

"Figure?" said Claude confused.

"There!" I said and pointed to the lit frame high up towards the upper gables.

"You see him? Please Claude tell me you see as I do!"

I watched as Claude narrowed his eyes and focussed upon the house.

"Yes, yes I do see him. Why, surely that is just Baxter my dear?" said Claude, wondering why I should make such a thing out of nothing, but he did not know as I did. He did not know that the window looked outwards from a room that did not exist, not in a natural sense.

"Tell me, have you ever been in that room? Do you even know how to find it?" I asked.

Claude looked at me with a puzzled expression as though I had just bamboozled his brain with an impossible question. He glanced back up at the window, at the figure.

"Yes, I-I think so, no. You know, it is the damnedest thing, for I cannot think of it."

"You cannot think of it because it does not exist!"

"Does not exist?" he repeated, still confused.

"Look, I know what I am about to say will sound absurd, especially to you but I have every reason to believe that the figure in the window is your Uncle Laurence!"

"What?"

"I have not taken leave of my senses; you must believe me Claude. I-I do not understand how but he still exists, in this house, in a room that should not be there."

After I said it, I instantly felt foolish. Claude placed both his hands on my shoulders.

"You are unwell. I should fetch for the doctor, he …" I pulled away and ran to the house.

"Come on, I will show you," I said, and he came after me, urging me to slow down, fearful I might slip on the wet grass.

Inside the house I made a course for the upper storey within the wing of the house that had been *forsook* by the family. With Claude close at my heels and with my skirts hoisted for speedy ambulation ,I feared I could trip and fall at any moment but I had to get there, to the room. We passed Baxter on the staircase, and he watched in alarm as we climbed in a whirlwind of urgency. I knew the room itself was like an ephemeral dayfly flaunting its brief existence, only to withdraw back into the darks from where it remained undetected. I followed the same path as I had during the night of the party, and I imagined that I could again see that buoyant shadow like a wreath of fog as it curled around the corners always out of reach, only to eventually fade from my view and blend with the other shadows.

Exasperated, I stood and faced a blank wall as Claude caught up with me. We were both heavily perspiring from our exertion. I hammered the wall with my fists and cried out in frustration.

"Show me!" I yelled, and Claude gently covered my fists with his hands.

"Please Bella, stop you will hurt yourself," he said.

"The room *was* here it was I tell you. You must believe me!" I wailed but I knew it was futile. I relented and sank to my knees as I watched Claude look upon me with a mix of fear and concern. Baxter too now stood beside him and puffed like an old engine, and I thought in that moment he may suffer a coronary. He was well past middle age and I realised then how he must have struggled to carry me, the night I fainted, all the way to my room; it must have almost killed him.

"There is no room here my lady, there simply could not be. You see this is an external wall, beyond which is a fifty-foot drop," added Baxter, and I looked at the wall. I had felt how cold it was to the touch and I somehow knew Baxter was right but how was it that I had once entered that room? I surely must have stood upon a carpet of air as I perused that almost devilish space. It was impossible, yet it happened.

"My love, you worry me so," said Claude, as he

helped me rise to my feet.

I fought the tears that welled in my eyes borne from being so mercilessly foiled (by the *house*) and to make matters worse, in front of both my husband and the butler. Realising how the whole scene must look I quickly pulled myself together and dismissed my actions, blaming them on my condition which was causing me to feel emotionally fragile and scatty. I knew that men would accept and not question such a response and I was right. Soon I was being carefully guided back downstairs amongst such cossetting that threatened to test my already frayed nerves.

Claude sat with me in the drawing room; he had ordered tea and as we waited for it to be brought to us Henry and Dorothea entered. It was obvious to both that Claude and I were not ourselves; we were having a quarrel over Claude insisting that a doctor be called to the house. Poor Baxter was sent backward and forward in and out of the room as first Claude would order him to send word to the family physician only for me to dismiss the instruction. I was adamant that it was unnecessary and claimed that all the recent events were a product of the feminine condition of being with-child.

"I shall cancel my trip to Thebes," said Claude.

I implored him not to because I knew how much the work meant to him and I would never forgive myself for being the one to steal away such an eminent opportunity. It was then that Henry asked us both what on earth the matter was. Claude updated his parents with the discomfiting details. I saw how Henry looked at me and I was ashamed because it appeared, I had so blatantly disregarded his wishes. I then felt that I had to say something, but Henry spoke first.

"I need to share something with you Arabella," said Henry, and he sat on a small settee and was joined by Dorothea. As he spoke, Dorothea held his hand and watched Henry with eyes that were filled with worry borne from concern for her husband.

Henry spoke of a time when Claude was but an infant, a time when Star Lake was plunged into uncertainty after Laurence's disappearance remained unresolved. I sat and listened quietly with Claude by my side; it seemed Henry was clearly opening up about all the things I wanted so desperately to hear about.

"The whole devilish business put us all on edge, we became … overly sensitive. I myself became unwell as I succumbed to the atmospheres within the house," said Henry, and I watched as Dorothea gently squeezed his hand. He smiled at her as she stroked his hand to tell her that he was fine, as though just talking to me would revive some of his past affliction.

"Death had once fallen like a midnight shadow upon Star Lake and the old family that once lived here. When that happens, sometimes old places like this somehow retain emotions, feelings that never truly fade. I once thought as you do my dear, that I had in fact found a room within Star Lake, an old room, filled with shadows of the past. I had been drinking heavily at the time with all the worry over my brother. I was not myself and I allowed the moods of the house to pierce my sensibilities and I suffered for it."

Henry then went on to say how he *thought* he saw *something* which I postulated must have been *the room*. Henry put his experience down to being part of his malady.

"It was nothing real, nothing tangible. I had a breakdown, a complete nervous collapse. Dorothea nursed me back to health, but it took time. I do not wish the same thing for you my dear, if you are feeling fragile; do not let an old place like this take hold of your senses. It is best to let it go."

As Henry finished speaking, I noticed that Viola had come to loiter in the doorway behind Baxter. When she saw that I had spotted her she quickly departed, leaving only the rustle of her dress to occupy the space she once filled. Baxter, to his relief was finally dismissed, and he left the room closing the doors behind him.

Again, I had to promise Henry that I would not look for the mysterious room and once more I lied to him. How could I simply let this go? There was a mystery here that needed answers. It was more than just a nervous malaise because people, actual people, had periodically gone missing and never returned. I myself had been into the room and what I experienced was tangible and real, whether an echo from the past or not. At least three of us including Laurence have experienced … something, our talking about it or the act of writing things down in old poetry books has corroborated each other's experience. I do not believe any of us were or *are* mad. We found something real.

For Henry's sake, and for Claude, I said that I would henceforth dismiss it all from my mind and never go wandering within that part of the house again. They were all happy with my answer, and I artfully changed the subject several times to lighten the mood and to quell any further suspicions they may have had regarding the integrity of my promise.

**

Before I had left Kitty at Holly Lane House, she asked me if I would see to it that a parcel with two letters were sent in the post to Ireland. It had not been her intention to remain with my parents when I returned to Star Lake and the letters included some birthday wishes and a gift for her Grandmother. I said that I would ensure they were dispatched in time, and one evening when the family all seemed to be otherwise occupied, I slipped down to Kitty's room.

It was a dark night; clouds had masked the

moon and all the rooms and passages were filled with the light from lamps or fires. The glow from the lamps upon the polished woods of the walls and the furnishings, helped to lighten even some of the darkest corners. I carried my own lamp and found Kitty's room and used a small key she had given me to unlock her door.

It was cold inside as there had not been a fire to warm the interior for several days and the spiders had been industrious with their webbing between the trims of the open drapes. I went over to the small writing desk that Kitty had described and raised the lid. Inside was a pair of enveloped letters bound by ribbon which rested upon a small oblong parcel wrapped in brown paper. I took them out and it was then that I heard a jangle from behind and I turned to see that the door handle was being rattled. The door was unlocked and yet it was as though someone on the other side was struggling to enter *or trying to be a nuisance.*

"Hello? Who is there?" I called out.

I received no answer and the whole situation was beginning to frighten me.

After I called out a second time, I heard a voice, and the words were formed from breath alone, it seemed to be hissing as it spoke a name.

'*Kitty,*' it sputtered.

Alarmed I inserted the key and locked the door. There was a split in one of the door panels and I cautiously placed an eye to it so that I could observe who, or *what* was on the other side. I saw a flash of white, a pallid face visible for an instant. I stepped back from the door when the pounding began. The handle continued to be twisted, turned, and rattled. My terror was building like the layering of coverlets one upon the other until I felt smothered by fear.

I watched horrified as the key was dislodged from the keyhole to fall to the floorboards as though poked out from the other side. I saw a pair of long fingers appear under the door where they scratched and rummaged until they found the small iron key. The fingers and the key disappeared and then I heard it being inserted into the lock from the other side. I reached up to the chimney piece and gripped hold of a long brass candlestick and I held it as one wields a weapon, to use on whatever *creature* was about to enter the room.

The hinges growled as the door was slowly pushed inwards.

"Esther?" I called, remembering the name upon the child's grave near the chapel. Why I called her name I did not know, it was more of an intuition than anything solid. After calling out her name it was as though my utterance had arrested whatever, or whoever was about to enter. The rattling of the handle stopped. The whispering voice became silent.

"Esther," I repeated. "Esther … is that you?"

Suddenly I felt brave, and I reached out and

wrenched open the door. A woman almost toppled inwards before releasing her grip on the door itself. When she straightened her posture, I could see that she was wearing a mask, the same mask I had seen hanging on a hook in Viola's room. I snatched it from her face and saw Viola's startled eyes, growing wide as saucers as she let out a surprised cry and scurried out of the room. Her nightgown was glowing in the candlelight as she ran away and gave the appearance of the ghost she had tried to be.

I attempted to follow, calling to her to stop running, to face me as my old fear had now turned to anger. It was clear to me that it was Viola who had been Kitty's tormentor and not a spirit as she had believed. I followed her all the way to her own room where she darted inside and secured the door. Using my fists, I hammered upon it and demanded that she come out to face me; alas, her door remained closed, and she did not answer. Annoyed and somewhat thwarted I took a walk up to Claude's observatory.

Chapter VIII
And then there were three

Although what Viola had done to Kitty was truly unforgivable, I now felt the combined emotions of guilt and sorrow for Viola's fate. I had imagined nothing more than a severe scolding from her parents with perhaps any allowances she enjoyed halved or removed during a period of reflection for what she had done. Her punishment however was harsher than that. She was to be sent away to stay with an aunt she detested, Dorothea's sister, for an indeterminant stretch of time. Viola was appalled and pleaded with her parents but Henry seemed adamant that she had to go. In the end she had accepted her father's wishes and had spent the days leading up to her departure full of gloom.

Of course, I knew that Viola's performance in faking Star Lake's ghost did not resolve all the *otherworldly* problems at all. Despite everything, there was the elusive room, the mysterious figure of a man at the window, the china dolls that tend to crop up most unexpectedly, and the shadow-like forms I had seen around the house. All these somewhat disturbing matters still required explaining, and it seemed as though only I had the desire to do so.

It was Viola's last day at Star Lake before she left for Norwich. The mood of the day fitted her sombre disposition. It was a dim light neither day nor night as the gloom of the dawn brooded well into the afternoon. I was out walking when I came across her; I saw her from a distance and she walked tiredly, in a moping way with a slumped posture and her head bent as she kicked about the leaves that had once adorned the oaks around her. She did not hear my approach, or if she did, she showed no interest or need for company. I greeted her in a friendly way and for a second, she glanced at me, and a brief smile spread from her lips before it was wiped away by the wind's breath.

"Viola, I intend to speak with your father. I am sure I can convince him that no real harm was done, and you can stay here at your home, where you belong," I said.

Viola replied without looking at me; instead, she continued to kick at the leaves until her shoes were quite soaked from their slippery dampness.

"Thank you but you know how Papa is, nothing can change his mind when it is set, not you, or I or even Mama."

"Oh, but I feel so dreadfully sorry. Ever since I

came here, I seem to have caused you nothing but trouble which I never intended to do."

"I know and I do not blame *you*. It is not you, or Papa. It is this place. Star Lake," she said, glancing up at the lofty gables. "I apologise for what I have done, to the Iri … to your maid. I now know it was wrong but it was not my desire, to do those awful things. I had to do it. *She* wanted me to do it."

"She? Who wanted you to do it? What do you mean?" I asked, somehow knowing the answer already.

"I told you this place had a ghost did I not? It was her house before, and it is still hers now."

"Esther?" I asked.

"Yes. That is her name. I see you have visited the chapel?"

I told her I had.

"You see, ever since I had my accident, when I broke my arm near the dead trees, she has always come to me. Mama called her my '*Make-believe*' friend. If only she was just that, but she has remained remarkably persistent for a child's pretend friend considering I am almost a grown woman!"

"How does she come to you?" I asked and wondered if Viola had dreamt the same dream as I had done my entire life.

"She just does, in many ways. Not all of them are easy for me to explain. *She* … tells me to do things, I have to obey, I simply must! I fear that if I do not, then she will do it herself, and the games, the silly stupid games will become something else, something other than mere amusements. It would be far too terrible to imagine."

Viola looked a little afraid as she told me these things; it was almost as though she feared for her family now that she would no longer be amongst us. I wondered if she had ever seen the room itself, or if she had ever been inside. I was about to ask her when Nellie appeared, and she called for Viola. We waited for her to join us.

"Pardon me m'lady, I was sent to fetch you. Watson is now ready with the coach. His Lordship and Ladyship are waiting to say goodbye."

"Thank you, Nellie. Please tell them I shall be with them presently," said Viola, and we watched her tramp back through the long-wet grass towards the house.

"Papa thinks the change of scenery will do me good, but I know I will hate it. My Aunt's house is such a drab place, and I will have to endure my bothersome cousin George too."

"I heard Claude talking with your mother and it seems that George is becoming quite the gentleman," I said, hoping to add a little sanguinity to the whole affair.

"I seriously doubt that very much, but I shall tease him as much as he attempts to harass me. You can mark my words on that score," she said, and this time her smile began to resurface as she left me to walk back between the oaks, following the trail Nellie had made through the morning dew that still lingered like beads upon the coverlet of the earth.

The day eventually yielded to the early blue light and later the family sat together in the drawing room for the first time without Viola. Claude was the first to speak about her departure saying how his Aunt would be a good influence upon her, but I recalled her solemn face staring back at us through the coach window as she was driven away from Star Lake.

"She has always been a little highly strung, brooding around the place for years," said Henry, as he sat wearing one of his Indian silk smoking suits whilst enjoying a Cuban cigar.

"I shall miss her terribly," said Dorothea, and she poured herself a second glass of sherry.

"Would you play for us?" she asked, and I accepted the invitation and made my way over to the piano.

"Oh, no, would you mind playing the harpsichord my dear, it will remind me of my dear little girl," she asked.

I seated myself at the instrument and played a sensitive piece to reflect the mood about the house that evening. Dorothea smiled as I played, and she occasionally used a handkerchief to dab at the corners of her eyes.

Outside a fresh wind had gained strength and it announced its arrival as though it was a parading band. The windowpanes rattled under each blast and the wind's gusting chorus attempted to drown out my own melody. On a piano it is possible to play louder or quieter by striking the keys with more or less force, but the harpsichord was unlike a piano and in the end, I was forced to stop playing.

"Here come the winter winds!" announced Henry. "A little early this year. I shall have to think about protecting my *Nepenthes*," he said, and I remembered the carnivorous plants of which Henry was so fond. Claude walked over to the windows and peered outside, and I joined him. The moon was bright, so bright, and under its light we could both see the trees bending and swaying outside as though the wind was determined to wake them early from their slumber before spring arrived. The lawns looked frosty and silvery, and I thought of the painting, Laurence's painting that now sat on my easel in my art room and I wondered if the house would now look like that picture bathed in the moonlight.

I was feeling fatigued more than usual these past few weeks and the family doctor had attributed this to my pregnancy. I was worried that the howling winds would keep me awake during the night and add to my now usual daily lethargy, so I decided to retire early. Claude said that he would join me shortly and I slowly climbed the staircase to our bed chamber. My thoughts about the painting earlier induced me to look upon it as I walked by the door to my atelier. I entered and saw the easel still covered by a sheet. I removed the cover so I could see the picture and at once I saw it, the window. I was sure that it had never been part of the picture before and there was something else; there was a figure painted in the window. As I looked at the figure, I saw how it glistened under the light from the lamp I carried as though the paint was still wet. With a timorous hand I reached out and touched it and my finger smudged the figure. I looked at the paint on my fingertip and then I saw the brush resting upon the top canvas holder. I picked it up and saw that there was fresh paint on the tip, wet paint.

I was right about the wind, the serenade of winter. For most of the night, its persistent whining and howling disturbed my sleep. In the morning when I had my breakfast tray brought by Nellie, I was almost too fatigued to eat. Claude was worried as he usually is but once I was up and dressed and had taken some of the cool crisp air, I was soon feeling more alert.

Before I took my morning walk, I had sent word to Kitty at Holly Lane House by way of a letter, telling her of the recent developments regarding Viola and that she should now at least feel at ease to return to Star Lake. Claude's valet, Fergus offered to post it for me. I also let Mrs Dexter know that I had sent for her. She fixed me with her steely eyes but after we had a brief chat, I could see that her promise to work Kitty harder on her return had been forgotten.

It was not just the winter winds that had started too soon this year. It was only early November and yet the frosts had begun. The lawns were stiff and white, and the otherwise stark trees were blooming with winter's blossom. It was the first step back into the chill of winter and I had taken to wearing a quilted cape with a fur lined hood to keep warm during my walks, and my hands were kept snug wrapped in a fur muff. It was peaceful and quiet as a cold winter morning usually is, the only sound was the crunch of frost under each of my steps as I came upon Henry's glass house.

I could see movement within, and I peered past the fern frosts upon the many little windows and saw Henry inside with one of the groundsmen. I glanced over to where the summer house stood enclosed by the dead trees. I shivered as I recalled my dream, whereupon entering the dark structure a phantom shadow had sat weeping on the floor clutching a broken china doll, and then she had reached out for me in such a terrifying manner that my flesh, if it had not been a dream, would have quaked because of it. I averted my gaze from that neglected pitiful place, no longer wanting to recall the dream, and again looked into the glass house. Henry had moved off somewhere else and I saw that the door was slightly ajar. I was chilled, so I slipped inside.

I walked amongst the plants noticing how some had turned brown or black and others had become brittle as old dead leaves crispen. The *Nepenthes*, Henry's rather odious carnivorous plants did not appear to be suffering under the recent cold spell. The colours were as fresh and as vibrant as when I had first seen them during the summer. I recalled how humid it had been to stand in the glass house, yet now on the cusp of winter I needed capes and muffs, and woollen stockings to keep warm.

I saw one of the *Nepenthes* cup-like appendages bulging and pulling heavily upon the stem. As I looked at it closely it seemed to quiver as though something struggled from within. I withdrew one of my hands from the muff and gingerly with a finger lifted the lidded cap and saw to my horror a small field mouse trapped inside. The mouse was jerking weakly but was it still alive or was it merely some action of the plant itself? I remembered Henry's explanation of his plants:

'The insides of the cup are slippery, and the prey are unable to climb back out— they are slowly dissolved in the liquor within, a kind of chemical teeth.'

I could not stand the thought of something alive being eaten so slowly so I found a twig and I tried several times to scoop out the mouse, but it was as though the plant had a firm hold of it and was not prepared to lose its prize.

After many more attempts I realised that I was now causing damage to the plant, but I stopped only when I heard Henry and another man re-enter the space where I stood amongst the miniature jungle. I dropped the twig temporarily leaving the mouse to its fate and stood straight, as erect as I could considering my increasing baby-bump. Henry saw me and smiled as he approached. He was carrying his coat over an arm and his sleeves were rolled up exposing two begrimed hands and forearms covered by smut streaks.

"My dear Bella, what brings you over to my glasshouse on such a cold morning?" he said, before dismissing the other man, equally as tarnished as he was.

"I don't know, I expect I needed the walk, to blow away the cobwebs from a restless night," I answered.

"The wind has run out of breath, the calm after the storm it would seem," he said.

He asked me to follow him as he wanted to show me something. I was led towards a large iron structure not unlike the front end of a steam locomotive. Thick copper and iron pipes ran off it and merged with others I had seen, filling the void of the glasshouse without ever wondering before what their purpose was. Henry explained that many years ago he had installed a boiler and heating system fuelled by coke and was very proud of his work showing me every pipe, bar, cog, and pin. He explained how he used it to keep his plants alive during the winter months; all I could think about as he talked was the field mouse still trapped, still being 'slowly dissolved – by the chemical teeth.' I thought about how wretched it had looked with greasy blackened fur and dull red eyes.

Once Henry had grown tired of showing me his creation, he began to stoke the boiler becoming enthralled in adjustments to pressures and the waters within the system itself. I wandered away where I intended to resume the task of freeing the mouse but try as I might I could no longer see that bulbous fleshy-pink cup. I searched among the plants, within the knots of tendrils yet I could not find it. It was almost as though the plant had concealed it from me. It was a ludicrous idea, the very thought that a plant could even think such a thing. I left the glasshouse just as the heat began slowly to radiate from the pipework and was feeling despondent in my failure to rescue the mouse from its fate worse than death.

***

It was a pleasant surprise one morning towards the end of the week when Kitty appeared in my room carrying a breakfast tray. It transpired that she had taken a coach from Holly Lane House to Star Lake the previous evening. We greeted each other affectionately and as Claude was already up and dressed and no doubt tinkering in his turret, she sat herself on the end of the bed. She talked about how she had loved being at Holly Lane House, and how it felt like, "A proper home."

It seemed both my parents had become attached to Kitty and she to them.

"I didn't like to leave your parent's place m'lady, but I couldn't leave you without a maid, not in your condition," she said. "I must admit I was afraid to come back but your letter told me everyt'eng I needed to know about de terrible business with Miss Viola. What a wicked woman she is too!"

Kitty handed me a little package wrapped with brown paper and tied with a blue ribbon.

"Your mum sent you a little gift."

I took the package and untied the band. Once the paper was removed, I could see that it was a book of baby names. The endearing little book delighted me, and I pictured my mother as she had no doubt perused the books within the modest bookshop in the village, thinking of me and finally selecting this very book which I now held in my hands. Kitty left me with my breakfast tray and as I ate, I flicked through the book and the list of names, both boy and girl, seemed endless. The names were taken from places, and nature, or colours and virtues: *Patience, Faith, Violet, Olive, China, Pearl.* I had never thought about how many names there could be as families like mine or Claude's usually reused names from relatives or direct ancestors. My mother, for example, was the third Amelia of her own family line.

Breakfast was soon forgotten as I became captivated by the choices registered in the book but then a bird collided with the windowpane in my room with such force as to leave a greasy imprint. Startled by the sound it made, I dropped the book but quickly recovered it from the floor only to find that my clumsiness had caused a casualty, a page was bent and almost torn from the top right-hand corner of the book. As I tried to straighten the paper, I noticed that the name sheared by a tear was Esther. A coincidence I thought as I tried to fool myself; nothing more than a fluke, a quirk. I read the description of the name *Esther* that the book provided.

"*Esther is derived from the Old Persian word stāra, meaning star, in the Old Testament.*"

A fitting name for a girl living in a place named Star Lake Hall I thought as I closed the book but the damage to that single page was now preventing a tidy seal.

The garden looked lovely dressed in winter's frock. A sturdy coating of frost stiffened the landscape. The hardened grass creaked beneath my feet as I decided to bear the chill and find a spot to sit outside and to paint the house as Laurence had once done. As I sat and sketched Star Lake in my art book, I wondered if Laurence had worked in the darkness under the moonlight, or had he simply converted his image from day to night later whilst working in the warmth of the house. I shall never know but he had managed to capture the light from the moon so beautifully as it highlighted the trees and fell upon the rooftops of the hall, and I liked to imagine that he *had* positioned himself where I now sat.

My hands were becoming numb as I began to add colour to my drawing and my little glass of water into which I dipped my brushes to clean them was beginning to ice over. I was about to stop painting and go back indoors because I had lost too much feeling in my hands, but I then saw the window. It hung again between the central gables and the weak light from within the room itself yielded the same silhouette of whom I had come to believe to be Laurence. Quickly, I added the window to my painting as rain began to spot the paper. I looked up at the darkening sky where the clouds were gathering, and the icy rain mixed with hail began to fall heavily washing the frost away beneath my feet. I completed the window and then I do not know why I had not done so before, but I felt the impulse to signal to the figure that stood as ever so motionless.

I raised my arm and waved and then I watched in horror as the form slowly lifted an arm in a weak response and seemed to place a hand upon the glass. Thunder grumbled overhead and the rain was now washing my painting from the paper. I did my best to cover it as I made my way back to the house. There was no surprise when a final glance up to the window revealed that, like my own painting, it had disappeared, as though cleaned away by the rain.

Claude was concerned when he saw my bedraggled wet form. We met on the stairs as I hurried to our room to remove my soaked garments.

"How can I go away to Thebes and leave you here when you do not look after yourself?" he said angrily.

I knew his annoyance was borne out of concern, so I paid no mind to his growl. I told him not to be silly and that I was merely caught in the rain as I took my morning walk. He called for Kitty and instructed her to draw me a warm bath.

As I lay in the bath, I stroked my stomach with one hand and held the book of baby names in the other. For amusement I searched for all the names of those I knew to see if the meanings of the name had had any influence on their own character or nature.

My own name, Arabella meant, *'An answered prayer'* or, *'Beauty in all ways'* or so the book said. Claude's was somewhat obscure as the book described the meaning to be, *'Of Latin origin'*, denoting, *'Lameness or absence'*. I had to smile due to the irony, for although I loved Claude to the very core of my being, he was in fact absent so much from my company and would soon be even more so in Thebes. Laurence signified, *'A state of peace'*, and I wondered if that was how he felt confined amongst the other shadows in that intangible room. Is that why he stood facing the window in order to see the life outside, the life he once lived? To Kitty was ascribed, *'Cute and adorable'*, and I could not think of a better matched pair of attributes. Viola was assigned, *'Curious and impulsive'*, and *'A free-spirited individual'*.

I then returned to the entry for Esther, it was easy to find as the book, now due to its injury, always fell open to that page. *'Esther is derived from the Old Persian word stāra, meaning star'*. I wondered if her parents had named her *Esther* after the house or was it merely happenstance? As I lay back in the warm water I thought about the name, Star Lake Hall. It seemed like a cold name, conjuring up visions of cool dark waters sprinkled with the reflections of stars. *'Ancient suns'*, Claude had called them; suns so far away as to give no warmth. There is a lake, I have walked along its banks where the willows with their graceful arching branches droop to kiss the water. I had sat and watched the dragon and damsel flies hover upon the reeds and the lilies floating upon the dark water like white stars. It was an enchanting place in summer but in wintertime, under the moonlight, preserved beneath a sheet of ice, it would feel like a different place altogether.

DAVID RALPH WILLIAMS

***

The day came when Claude finally left for
Thebes. It was an emotional departure for the
whole family. Claude made a promise to write me
a letter as often as he could until his return to
Star Lake in December. He waved at me from the
windows of the coach as it departed, and I could
see that his face was burdened with melancholic
thoughts as he was driven along the path and
finally out of sight. I instantly felt bereaved and
became tearful and was taken inside by Henry
and Dorothea.

There were only the three of us now as family, and Dorothea had taken to spending a lot of
time in my company probably because Claude had
asked her to watch over me, and maybe because
she missed Viola too. As the days went by, we sat
by the fireside; Dorothea would be at her needle-
work whilst I would add colour to my paintings. It
had become too cold to sit outside so I relied upon
my colour sketches and now mixed my paints to
match the colours I had replicated whilst out in
the natural light. Since the morning a bird had
struck my bedchamber window, there had been
no other odd occurrences. All seemed quiet and
uneventful within Star Lake but that was about to
change.

Chapter IX
The Christmas Room

It was the season of short days and bitterly cold nights. As I retired to bed one chilly evening, all was silent as a winter's night usually is. I had been troubled by dreams since Claude had left for Thebes, but this night was particularly bad. In my dream I found myself walking within the burnt ruins of Star Lake as though the house itself had suffered a terrible catastrophe. As I walked, I could smell smouldering woodwork and felt that I was not quite alone as a thing without substance trailed me, always keeping to the channels of shadow. Whatever, or whoever it was had projected enough of its presence upon me to cause my heart to shudder, my skin to bristle, and my thoughts to be cast down undesirable paths to where danger lurks in the darkness.

I turned a corner where the roof was now gone, and the stars were visible overhead. I realised I was standing in what was left of my atelier. Laurence's painting still rested upon the easel, but it had changed. No longer was it a house standing gaunt beneath the moonlight; now it depicted a burning inferno as flames licked blue-black skies and thick smoke eclipsed the moon. I reached out to pick up the painting to examine it and as my hands gripped the framed canvas another pair of hands, cold and hard clasped around my own.

Anyone who has ever experienced being seized by a *ghost* in a dream will tell you how fearful they are of being in the presence of one after they have woken. The sensation of the cold hands wrapping themselves around my own in the dream was so powerful that when I woke with a jolt, I could feel that I was under the watchful gaze of another's *presence* in the room. I sat up in my bed and called out.

"Who's there?"

Nobody answered and neither did I expect an answer because dreams, when broken do not answer, or so I thought.

Before I went to sleep, I had left the window uncovered so that I could search for the pair of stars that Claude had likened to our twin souls shining brightly within the night sky. The moonlight had flooded my room and had come to rest at the foot of the bed. I could now see the shape of a child as she stepped out of the gloom and her dark eyes cast an icy gaze upon me. Her face was caught under the moonlight reflecting a shadow-daubed, marble white pallor. Her tissue thin skin was stretched across her skull forming creases that resembled the fine lines often seen upon the faces of porcelain dolls. She glided effortlessly away from my bed and towards the door where she beckoned with a clandestine signal and although terrified, I was compelled to follow.

After a long journey through the darkened house, I found myself again standing before that impossible door. Moments earlier I had watched as the corpse-like form of the girl, still beckoning me to follow her had melted before it, disappearing completely. I gripped the handle; it was cold, so cold. I could see the blinking light from underneath the door cast I was sure, from the weak fire within. I could hear the dim notes of the harpsichord playing out from somewhere far below, the old Christmas carols played in a mournful key. I turned the handle and opened the door.

The first things I noticed were the lush garlands of greenery strung about the room trailing corner to corner. I could smell the warm bright aroma of Christmas holly and pine, and seasonal spices, the aroma of Christmas itself. A feeble fire skipped in the grate and candles positioned about the hazy room cast hardly enough light to cut through the shadows. Standing again in this room felt like a blatant defiance of a natural law. Purposefully leaving the door ajar I stepped further inside, and with every footfall the room began to open to me as the mists receded, and the ghostly forms once again began to surface. Some of the figures were not as clearly discerned, almost out of frame but others were sharper, crisper.

The shadows about the room mostly seated and darkling as ghosts, now had substance and faces that had that vivid glow usually captured in many an old painted portrait set upon a dark background. They were all dressed in outdated attire. The men wore wigs and ruffles about the wrists; the women were dressed in chemise gowns and donned neckerchiefs. The ghostly occupants were now beginning to perceive my arrival and they glanced palely at me where I stood and like the eyes of such old paintings, they followed me as I moved with trepidation amongst them, regarding me through the mists of eternity. Could they see me? How did I appear to them? Am I the one with a face of woe and gloom-ridden eyes?

*The shadows about the room mostly seated
and darkling as ghosts,
now had substance and faces that had that
vivid glow usually captured in
many an old painted portrait set upon a dark background.*

There was food laid out on tables and some of the *people* were eating but the food was spoiled and magots writhed within each forkful as it was devoured by the phantoms seated around the tables. At a small desk two men were playing chess and I could hear an audible clack as the chess pieces were placed down upon the polished wood. There was a clock on the mantle whose pendulum had frozen in mid swing, and I realised then that within this room there are no hours, there is no time. I stood in a placeless timelessness, in a room filled with the whispering voices of the past. This scene of Christmas had somehow impressed itself upon the hidden emotional heart of the house, as all the Christmases of yore had re-

159

turned to haunt this space.

I continued to watch as the figures opened their mouths as though speaking to one another, yet I could not hear the words they uttered, and as their mouths mutely formed the inaudible speech, they issued what I first thought was a froth, or a rabid foam, and then I saw that it was in fact ice that flowed from their mouths, a fine powdered snow, spilling onto their gowns and coats, spreading upon the tables. Finding this aspect unsettling I looked away to the corners of the room still dark and in shadow. I then saw the familiar form of a man at the window, again with his back turned to the room and his gaze stolen by the view outside; the richly wooded landscape beyond captivating him.

I knew that, should I be stood outside of the house gazing upwards, then I would see him as the silhouette that has haunted me since my arrival at Star Lake. Here in the room, I could see him in vivid colour, wearing a fine silken hat and coat of plum velvet studded with golden buttons on the backs of the sleeves. I approached the man and as I drew closer, I whispered his name.

"Laurence," I said, and he appeared to flinch, and I was about to repeat his name, but his hand shot out and gripped my own. Suddenly fear had shrunk me making me feel small and weak. I tried to pull away from his grip, but he was too strong, and his hand was so cold like the hands I had felt in my dream, hands that had appeared from behind his own painting.

I continued to struggle and plead for release, but my words were now mere breaths. Suddenly he let go of me. Finally, I was free, but the fright wrung the scream from within me and I ran towards the open door that was slowly dimming and blurring. I almost fell to the floor as I reached the doorway but managed to stay upright clutching the architrave. I extruded myself from the room, but it took a great effort as I could feel a force that was binding itself to me and dragging me back inside. I turned and saw the spirits within growing darker, their eyes black with red pupils and their mouths agape and the fine powdered snow was tipping out like fine sand. I realised that they were all inhaling, and the combined force of their wasted translucent lungs was pulling me back, back inside as if I was nothing more than a tiny field mouse caught in one of Henry's disgusting plants.

It was then I felt my baby move inside me and my instincts to protect my unborn child came alive as I clawed my way away from the room. Now separated from the doorway and with my back to the wall outside I cried in terror and called for Claude even though he could not possibly hear me. Suddenly everything stopped. I prised myself from the wall and saw that the door had vanished, not a trace of it remained. I was still weeping when I heard footsteps behind me in the corridor. I turned to find Henry looking at me and he had anger in his eyes.

***

During the days that followed, I was always thinking of the room wherever I was, and wherever I walked the room was always with me. I had become infected by it. One morning I discovered that the servants had been ordered to create a barrier to block off the passage to the corridor that contained the *Christmas Room*. Baxter was with them, and I asked him why this was necessary.

"It is Lord Darlington's wishes My Lady," replied Baxter, and he then went on to explain how in the past there used to be an extra side to the house which had collapsed due to a problem with the foundations.

"The remaining side may still be unstable, and until we are in possession of the outcome of a report by a structural engineer, I have been ordered to see that the whole wing is sealed off," he explained. I wondered why this was never mentioned to me before. The fact that there *had* been an actual room beyond that wall, the ghost of which I had entered twice. Of course, I knew the real reason for the barrier, it was due to my blatant disregard for Henry's wishes. Now the whole area will remain closed off from the rest of the house, but I also knew that I would never venture to go into that room again.

I received my first letter from Claude that day and I carried it to the conservatory adjoining the library where I opened it to read the words my love had written. He wrote first about his journey to Greece and the fact that his ship almost sank due to high winds that forced the vessel to lean at perilous angles as the sea crashed upon it almost flooding it. He then went on to describe how the party, once ashore, began to set up the temporary observatory making use of one of the neglected temple ruins that sat upon one of the many mounts and hills.

'It is not overly hot but pleasantly warm as a May day in England, and we have around six hours of sun each day. The surrounding area has abundant springs of water and there is a small bustling market town providing all the necessary supplies we need.'

He then went on to describe how they had set up five small telescopes, chronometers (whatever they are), and a set of meteorological instruments. Finally, he concluded by saying how he was missing me.

'This letter may appear short but if I were to write a million pages, they would only repeat that I love you my dearest Bella, and I mark each passing day with a desire to be at home with you once again, my darling. Your constant, faithful, and affectionate true love, Claude.'

I carried that letter with me for the rest of the day missing him terribly.

The day after the barrier was constructed the house and grounds became steeped in the densest fog. I stepped outside briefly to take some air. The mist had thickened the cobwebs as they lay across the lawns and bushes, and I saw the blurred outlines of groundsmen as they moved like fish through murky waters, and it reminded me of the figures in the *Christmas Room* as I recalled their oddly transparent looks with their dark eyes and gaping mouths. Those memories were still fresh and raw and constantly flapped about inside my mind like trapped birds in an old turret. I began to feel afraid, and the fog started to clog my lungs, so I returned to the house. The fog stubbornly refused to lift before the hour fixed for luncheon.

As we dined, Henry was frosty with me as he had been since discovering me in the now sealed-off wing of the house. His responses to my small talk were curt and I saw how Dorothea had become concerned, troubled enough even to ask Henry what on earth the matter was. Henry simply glared at me and dabbed his mouth with a napkin before announcing he was going out riding.

"You are not serious? On a day like this? What about the horse?" asked Dorothea, with considerable anxiety.

"Monarch will be fine my dear, I often take him out in such murky weather; this fog is not like the

Blacks in London, it is country fog!" he said.

"Nevertheless, I think it would be foolish. Where do you intend on taking him?" she asked.

"Out through the woods where I always go."

"What if you should hit a low branch or—"

"I will be perfectly alright. Please my dear, enough of this fuss," said Henry, as he excused himself and made his way out of the room to get ready for his ride.

"I simply do not know what has come over Henry these past days, he is not like himself at all!" said Dorothea, and she looked to me hoping that I had some explanation, but I preferred to keep to myself the account of my wanderings and betrayal of Henry's trust.

"I expect he misses Claude," I said.

"Yes, you are probably right my dear, I also miss him as must you."

"Terribly," I replied.

It was almost early evening and dinner was delayed due to the absence of Henry who had not returned to the house since his departure around noon. The fog had refused to lift and in fact seemed to deepen, forcing the house to remain lamplit for the entire day. As I sat by the fire in the drawing room I watched as Dorothea paced up and down, often peering beyond the drapes at the window hoping for a sighting of Henry as he returned to Star Lake.

Since Henry had gone out riding the whole

house seemed to be submerged in a gloomy ambiance. I rose from my seat and using a fire iron I stirred the fire causing it to become brighter and cheerier.

"I am sure Henry is alright," I said, hoping to ease Dorothea's worries.

"It is just so unlike him to be out *so* long and in this dreadful weather!" she said, as she continued to peer out into the night.

It was almost an hour later when Baxter came into the drawing room wearing a face that was contorted into a mask of concern. Dorothea immediately knew that something was wrong, and we both stood to hear Baxter's news.

"I am sorry to have to tell you My Lady, but His Lordship's horse was found wandering amongst the stables about a half hour ago. There is no sign of His Lordship and Monarch was still wearing his saddle and bridle."

Dorothea put a hand to her mouth, and I quickly came to be by her side.

"Watson, with the groom and stable boy have gone out looking for His Lordship. I have also sent Douglas, Leo, and Hugh to the woodlands to see if they can help in the search. They have taken the hounds My Lady; I am sure we will have news soon."

"I told him not to go out in the fog, he wouldn't listen, he is so stubborn. Oh, what if something terrible has happened?" wailed Dorothea.

"I am sure that His Lordship is fine My Lady; I expect he tumbled from the horse and is slowly making his way back to the house, hampered by the murk outside I should expect."

"Oh, I do hope you are right. Please let me know as soon as there is any news will you."

"Of course, My Lady," said Baxter, as he left Dorothea with a glass of brandy to hold.

Later that evening Watson returned to the house to take the coach out. Henry had been found lying injured in the woods. The other men had stayed with him and when the coach returned to Star Lake, we saw them carefully carry Henry from the coach and he was placed into bed. Baxter went out to fetch the family doctor, and Dorothea and I remained with Henry as he rambled with delirium. He was obviously in so much pain for he kept on shouting out.

"My legs, I cannot move my legs!"

Dorothea tried unsuccessfully to calm him as he stared out from his bed with wild eyes not seeing us; it was as though he was searching for another.

"Keep her away from me, please for God's sake, keep her away," he wailed.

We were relieved when Baxter returned with the doctor and after a difficult but thorough examination the doctor concluded that Henry had suffered damage to his spine which had rendered him paralysed from the waist down. He had also sustained a broken arm and possible other damage to his neck vertebrae.

"Will my husband recover?" asked Dorothea, her voice quavering.

"I will give him something to put him out whilst I set his broken arm, it will be much easier than icing the limb. I am hoping that the fall has caused no serious or lasting damage to his spine, perhaps some swelling around the sensory tract is causing his paralysis. We shall know more in a few days."

As the doctor finished speaking Dorothea sat by Henry's bedside and she cried as the doctor forced Henry to drink a sleeping potion. He waited patiently for him to drop off before he worked on his arm which I could now see looked painfully crooked. I had to turn away as he manipulated the limb, as the sound of bone grinding upon bone was truly nauseating to bear.

The doctor left the house with a promise to return at first light. Henry was peacefully sleeping, and his arm was secure within its bindings. I intended to sit up through the night with Dorothea until the doctor returned but she insisted that I went to bed and got enough rest, if not for my sake, then for the child within me. Reluctantly I climbed the staircase to my bedchamber where I knew that sleep would not come easily. I sat up in bed and wrote a letter to Claude informing him of his father's accident. I would see that it was sent in the post first thing in the morning so that it had every chance of reaching him in the shortest time possible.

I woke early and parted the drapes in my room. It was a stark contrast to the murk of the previous day. The early morning sky blushed and was filled with winter embers. The doctor arrived as he had promised and was taken to Henry's room. There was no sign of improvement to his numbness, but it was only the morning after the night before. Again, I sat with Dorothea, as the doctor examined Henry. We were joined by Baxter and Mrs Dexter as the whole household were equally as concerned as we were. Fergus had taken my letter for Claude to the early post, and Dorothea had added one of her own for Viola.

For the rest of the day Dorothea and I took it in turns to sit with Henry. We tried to get him to eat which was difficult, but we made sure that he took sips of whatever drink Mrs Dexter brought up throughout the day. At one point I insisted that Dorothea take a nap as she looked so weary. She used a guest room for an hour or so and I sat with Henry and read some poetry to him from Laurence's book. From time to time, he would open his eyes and look at me as though checking it was indeed I who sat near him and not another.

The doctor had left some more potions for us to administer, and they had the effect of soothing Henry and helping him drift off to sleep. It seemed that the injury to his spine had left him unaware when he needed to visit the bathroom to relieve himself, and we waited for the potions to take effect before soiled bedsheets were carefully removed and replaced with clean ones. At one point when Henry was fast asleep Baxter came into the room to check on his master. We both spoke in hushed tones.

"According to Watson, they found him lying where he had fallen from Monarch, amongst the rotting branches and the fallen leaves, and Watson said that he wore an expression upon his face such as words could not describe, and he called out, '*The child!*' over and over," Baxter divulged. I noticed how as Baxter mentioned '*The child*,' Henry roused, and he opened his eyes to search about his bedchamber. I took up his hand and tried to shush him back to rest but he was agitated.

"She is here?" he said with wild eyes.

"No one is here, except Mr Baxter and I," I said softly.

"But I heard you speak of her, I heard … she … she had wild hair, wild and witchy!" shouted Henry. "She scared Monarch, she made him rear and kick and I fell. I … I could not rise, and she told me that she would take my family one by one, she tormented me, she, she …"

"He is speaking with delirium," said Baxter but I knew he was telling us what happened, speaking of her of Esther. I poured him a drink and tried to get him to sip it, but he just turned his lips from the cup and continued to babble. Baxter went off to find Dorothea and she came into the room looking as weary as she had before. She took up Henry's hand and she kissed it tenderly and stroked his brow and managed to soothe him back into slumber. I left them together.

***

There seemed little improvement to Henry's condition over the days that followed. It had almost been a fortnight and if anything, he seemed to deteriorate as though he was slowly fading away. Viola had come home, and she took up a permanent presence by her father's bedside. It was touching to see, and Viola herself seemed so very distant as though the sight of her father lying helpless in his bed had crushed her. There had been no word from Claude, and I wrote him another letter fearing the first may have become lost during its long journey across the seas. The daily visits from the doctor did nothing to aid Henry's recovery and his tones, when he spoke of Henry, were so very grave that all of those about his person fell quiet.

The local vicar of the parish called at the house to pay his respects to Henry. We told him how poorly Henry was and that he was not able to receive visitors, so we offered the vicar tea in the morning room. Viola as ever remained beside Henry's bed only joining our company during mealtimes, after which she would always resume her vigil. The Reverend John Haynes was extremely elderly and had lived in the area his whole life and had taken over the mantle of vicar from his father. He said how awful it was for the family to suffer such a misfortune and being so close to Christmas. I suppose that he saw our glum faces at the prospect, and he sought to lighten the mood by entertaining us both with tales of the old days.

"Oh, I remember one particular Christmas where all the butchers strove to win a local award of the best fat cow!" he said sipping his tea and chuckling to himself.

"How—interesting," said Dorothea, not really listening and still absorbed by her grief for Henry.

"What happened to the cow Reverend?" I asked respectfully.

"Oh, I suppose after it was fattened on corn stalks and bales of hay it was butchered and the meats hung, as they usually were, close to Christmas Eve. You see the fatted cow is merely a metaphor, a symbol of the festive celebrations and rejoicing for someone's long-awaited return. It stems from the fable of the Prodigal Son in the New Testament," he said, now enjoying a slice of slab cake.

"Of course, there was also the *wassailing!*" he added.

"Wassailing?" I asked.

"Oh, yes, it's not done very much these days sadly. The local manor house would fill a large bowl with spiced and sweetened cider and brandy, garnished with apples. The whole village would come out to drink the wassail, getting very *blootered!* Jugs of the stuff were taken around to those too old to leave their homes."

"It sounds very jolly," I said.

"Yes, yes it was my dear. It was the old belief that the *wassailing* was a way to scare away bad spirits and to wake up apple trees in time for the new year's harvest. Always popular about this town when I was a boy, and especially around here," he said frowning, as though he had found himself saying something he ought not to have said.

Dorothea excused herself saying she wanted to check on Henry. After she had left and I was alone with the vicar, I decided to ask him a direct question.

"What do you know about the previous family who lived at Star Lake?"

"Previous family? Only the Darlington's have ever inhabited—oh, unless you mean the original Darlington family; yes, a sad affair, very sad. Died of a pestilence that once blighted the countryside around these parts. I didn't know them you see because my father was the vicar then and I wasonly a boy myself. Now let me see, as far as I remember only Lord Darlington survived the scourge, that being the present Lord Darlington's grandfather. Why do you ask child?"

"I was curious. I saw the graves by the old chapel."

"Graves? Oh no, there are no graves. When Lord Darlington discovered that his whole family had succumbed to the sickness, he had their bodies burned and the ashes scattered somewhere on the estate, within a cluster of trees if I remember what my father said."

"Oh, but I have seen the graves, and they are clearly marked," I maintained.

"Well doubtless they are for appearances sake, it wasn't customary to burn one's entire family you know, not the *done* thing at all!" added the vicar, as he consumed a second slice of the slab cake.

It was with great joy the following morning that I finally received a letter from Claude. I felt a rush of relief the moment Kitty handed it to me along with my breakfast tray, and I could see by her expression that she was as thankful as I was upon its arrival. I tore it from the wrapper and speedily read Claude's words. Kitty watched almost bursting with anticipation until she could stand it no longer.

"Is it good news m'lady, is 'e coming back?" she asked excitedly.

"Yes, yes he is. The date on the letter is already over a week old, he should be home in days!"

I could hardly contain my delight and even in

my swollen state I sprang out of bed and both Kitty and I embraced and almost danced a pirouette.

"It's good dat 'e will make it back before 'is father—before 'is Lordship ... gets any worse." Kitty's grave words killed our cheerfulness as we both knew what she meant.

As I sat upon the bed to eat my breakfast Kitty began to speak of Viola.

"De woman seems out of it; she hardly speaks to me; never saying de awful cruel t'engs she used to say. She almost looks as if she is dreaming whilst she is awake! De oder day I found her in de morning room. I'd gone in to lay a fire for breakfast and she was just sitting in a chair, staring at de oder empty opposite chair. 'twas almost like she was listening to someone *talking* to 'er, and she often answered *'Of course'*, or *'At once'*; 'twas weird and it gave me goose pimples. After I'd lit de fire, she just sat and watched, and 'er usual slitty eyes were now big and round and filled with de dancing flames."

It was true what Kitty said, I had noticed the peculiarity with Viola myself, but I had simply put it down to the worry she must be feeling over Henry's worsening condition.

Later that night I was disturbed from sleep by the sound of shuffling outside my bedchamber door. I quickly put on my robe-de- chambre and investigated the source of the noise. I followed it along the passage only to find Viola wandering as if in sleep whilst carrying a lamp. I took it upon myself to guide her back to her own room, but the task was challenging. As soon as I had her almost to her chamber door, she would take off again as though following an imperceptible voice calling out from the unseen.

In the end, after I *had* managed to steer her to her bedchamber, I found the casement to be open and the cold wind rushing in where it had chilled the bedsheets. As I closed the window, I noticed a dim light slowly fading that appeared to be dancing far out amongst the dead trees. I covered the window with the drapes and attended to Viola, pulling the icy sheets to cover her and as I did, she gripped me tightly around the wrist. I struggled to break free, but her strength pulled me down close to her face.

"Get away from here," she whispered and then she released me. Somewhat shaken I rubbed my wrist and left Viola who now wriggled and writhed within her bed.

In the morning I was overjoyed when a coach arrived at Star Lake and Claude climbed out. I could not get outside quickly enough to greet him, and he was pleased to see me, his embrace told me that.

"Where is Father?" he asked.

"In his bedchamber but steel yourself my love," I said, forewarning Claude of the unpleasant sight that was to greet him inside.

I went with Claude and Dorothea to Henry's bedside, and I saw the pain in Claude's face as he saw his father lying broken under the blankets, with his eyes bulging wildly but not seeing, and his lip twisted and sagging as if pulled downward by an unseen hand. Henry merely coughed and gurgled at the sight of his son as though he was finally bereft of his senses.

"We shall find the best physician money can buy," Claude said, as he left the room casting one final glance at his father. Dorothea began to weep, and we both knew that no doctor, however accomplished, would be able to help Henry now.

***

Christmas was only weeks away but there was no joy in its coming at Star Lake Hall. Servants had tried to do their best to lighten the atmosphere and the house was decked with garlands of holly and evergreens and a Christmas tree was brought inside but the mood was still heavy and dark amongst the family. Kitty was unhappy at the premature yuletide trimming and adornment of the house saying it was considered unlucky in Ireland to bring greenery into the house before Christmas Eve.

Claude had appointed various physicians to attend his father, some coming from as far afield as Scotland or London, and all with their own unique ideas and contraptions but nothing they did could bring Henry back to us. Our own family doctor, feeling indignant, now focussed all his attentions onto me as the arrival date for the baby was fast approaching; it was the only thing that now brought joy to the household.

Chapter X
The shadow of time

It was Christmas Eve and snow fell thick during the afternoon; the large fat flakes covered the windows of the house darkening them well before the deep cold of night settled in. During the early evening there had been carol singers and Claude and I had resurrected the Wassailing tradition where jugs of spiced cider along with some other comestibles were taken by Watson and Oscar to the elderly in the nearby villages. Now late into the evening I sat in the drawing room with Claude and Dorothea; Viola had taken up her regular position at Henry's bedside.

There was a fire roaring in the grate and Baxter entered where he brought each of us a Christmas posset of hot spiced fruits.

"The house seems rather quiet this evening," said Dorothea to Baxter.

"Yes My Lady, it would seem that many of the household are in the village taverns, those who are willing enough to brave the worsening weather that is," he replied.

After our possets we retired to our bedchambers. I had always felt a tingle of excitement the night before a Christmas morning, yet now my feelings were a mixture of worry and disappointment. I had been so looking forward to my first Christmas at Star Lake ever since I had arrived, but I knew how solemn tomorrow's mood would be and nothing short of a miracle for Henry would be able to lift it. During the minutes before sleep, and thankful to be lying next to Claude, my thoughts were turned back to the *Christmas Room*, that space where Christmas was in perpetuity. The place where all those phantoms, those spirits, existed within its spell forever, never to experience again the burnished gold of a new dawn.

"*Fire!*"

A cry rang out. At first, I thought it to be a lingering element from an elapsed dream but then in a voice I recognised to be Baxter's, it boomed again.

"*Fire!*"

Now Claude was awake and shaking me and I opened my eyes as our chamber door was swung open and smoke billowed through. It looked as though it had been brushed by an artist's hand to highlight the invisible air in which it swirled around us. I could see Baxter's form standing in the doorway; he was coughing and covering his face with the sleeve of his dressing gown.

"The house is ablaze we need to get out!" he cried, and Claude was on his feet and helping me to mine and poor Baxter was almost collapsing under the darkening miasma.

"Is everyone out?" Claude asked anxiously.

"I have yet to find Her Ladyship or young Miss Viola; many of the servants are outside or are actively fighting the fire,"

"Good God, my father," cried Claude, angst-ridden.

"I am on my way to his room, but I will need help to carry him outside," said Baxter, his eyes red and streaming under the sting of the smoke. Claude looked at me and I realised that he was now torn between choosing who he was to help survive this disaster that was rapidly unfolding before us.

"Go with Baxter and hurry, I will be fine," I said.

"The staircase is free as the fire mostly rages on the far side of this floor," added Baxter, between attacks of coughing. Claude just stood there staring at me as the smoke rolled up and curled around all three of us.

"You must save your father," I implored.

Just then Kitty appeared in our room; she had her head covered with a bedsheet and held it up so that I could see it was her and hear her words as she spoke.

"T'ank God you are alright m'lady. Everyt'eng is going up. We must get out!"

"Kitty, please help Arabella to get outside," said Claude, and he kissed me.

"I will join you presently," he said, and he vanished with Baxter into the curtain of smoke. I took up Kitty's hand and she shared her coverlet and together we made our way to the main staircase.

As we descended, it became obvious that the fire had now spread to the lower floors; the golden glow and heat generated by the burning house around us became ever more intense. I saw how the leaping flames spread and burned in a fit of temper as though intensely angry at the house itself and the lives within it. Half covered by the sheet I could still smell the fire, taste it even, as everything was being consumed hungrily by it. It was then we saw her.

Viola was standing as though frozen amid the flames, her face almost a mask of indifference to the danger that surrounded her. She was holding a lamp and when she saw us her thin lips spread, and she smiled. I saw that her nightdress had caught fire and still she did not flinch. I called to her to follow us, and I pointed at her nightdress to draw attention to the fact it was burning. She paid no mind to my alarm. It was then, almost drowned by the roar of the flames that surrounded us, that I heard her speak.

"I will bury you all with fire as I was buried with fire. I am the moon that shines over this house lest anyone forgets."

I knew then that it was she who had started the fire, but the words spoken through her were not Viola's, they came from another. I stood and watched horrified as she raised the lamp she carried above her head and tipped its contents over herself. Instantly she was ablaze. I cried out in horror and was dragged away by Kitty.

The sight of the doorway was a great relief, the air was almost too smoky to breathe and now hot enough to scorch the skin. I turned to look for Claude and Baxter but all I could see were strangers as they rushed in and out of the house, many carrying buckets of water, some in uniform, but nothing could stand in the way of the flame's progress.

"M'lady, please we must get out!" cried Kitty, as she took a firmer grip of my hand.

"Claude, oh where is he, I can't see him, I—"

"'E will be alright m'lady I just know 'e will, now come with me before we both choke to death!" Kitty shouted, and she pulled me to reach the door. Soon we were both making our way across the snow-topped lawn with the sound of the flames and the cries of men, and the bursting glass of the windows behind us.

As we breathed the cooling air, and our lungs were rid of the burning fumes we stood and watched as the house burned. The fire brigade had arrived and were setting up their water engine with a pipe fed into the nearby frozen lake and men from the village and from the household were taking it in turns to pump the water as the firemen held the hose directing it towards the burning naked windows. Others had formed a long line and were filling buckets from the lake and were advancing them towards the house as the empty pails were returned. I could see no sight of Claude and my heart was in my mouth as I scanned every face that emerged from the blazing house.

Soon, other servants from the house, including Mrs Dexter and Nellie had joined us where we stood, and each one of us relieved to discover every survivor of the disaster that was still in progress. With each new face that emerged through the darkness covered by smuts I was becoming more and more alarmed by the lack of Claude, Baxter, Dorothea, or Henry. Finally, I saw two forms distorted by the heat as they stumbled from the flaming doorway; both were assisted by firemen who helped them towards where the rest of us had huddled. I was overjoyed to see Claude and Baxter as they slumped to the ground at our feet, poisoned from the smoke and weary from labour.

"I could not save them," said Claude as he looked at my face, his eyes streaming with tears.

"Mother refused to leave my father to die alone, their room was just burning sticks of charcoal when we eventually managed to break inside. I watched as they burned unable to help," he said, distraught.

"Oh my love, how they screamed through the fire, I shall never forget. Thank God, you are safe, I would never have forgiven myself, never."

I silenced Claude with a kiss and we both comforted each other as we silently watched the flames lick the walls from around the empty windows. Billowing smoke rose into the sky creating a blood-moon. Soon the roof was almost gone, collapsed inward and glowing sparks from the fire within spilled out and were cast into the sky reaching for the stars as though they were the heaven-bound souls of those who had perished.

"God love us, someone's still trapped inside look," cried Kitty. "We can't just leave de poor soul to burn to death!"

Claude and I followed her gaze and we saw the window to the *Christmas Room*, as ever illuminated from within and despite everything that was happening, the same dark profile of a man, like a rigid stain upon the glass, poised looking outward.

"We 'ave to tell someone, de firemen or—"

Kitty stopped speaking, scanning the house for the window that had now been snuffed out and snatched from her sight by the night and the smoke.

"I don't understand m'lady, 'e was dere, a moment ago, I swear 'e was."

Claude looked at me and we both understood what Kitty had seen.

"It must have been smoke in your eyes Kitty,"

said Claude. "If anyone *was* still in the house, they are already gone—lost," he added.

Everyone remained together to watch the house as it was destroyed by the fire. The firemen fought relentlessly to prevent the inevitable but when dawn finally arrived and the unfettered sunlight began to break free into the black winter morning the house was a shell, and the ground on which it stood was scorched and still that smell of burning, of bonfires lingered.

The days after the fire were painful for all who had once lived and worked at Star Lake Hall. Claude and I took up residence at Holly Lane House and Kitty came with us and my parents made all of us feel welcome and at home. A month after the fire we had our child, a beautiful baby boy whom we named Henry Laurence Darlington. He was the image of his father and became the apple of Claude's eye and stole all our hearts. Mrs Dexter and Baxter would occasionally come to visit until both had found new positions in houses up the country.

It transpired that both Claude and I inherited other properties near Norwich and London which had formed part of the Darlington estate but none as grand as Star Lake had been. We both felt so very much at home at Holly Lane that we decided to make this our permanent family residence. Claude had already purchased a patch of land upon a hillock and using some of the income we received from leasing the other properties, he began to construct a new observatory which he had sentimentally named *Star Lake Rise*.

***

The twelve months after the fire passed quickly and little Henry was already beginning to take his first tentative steps unaided. The start of Christmastide was now upon us again and the snow this year was unusually late, only just beginning to fall as I took Henry out for a walk before breakfast. When we both returned to the house the Yule Log was burning brightly in the hearth and wreathes of holly, lush with bright red berries decorated the house bringing colour to the darkest, gloomiest corners of time-blackened beams and brickwork.

Kitty had prepared drinking chocolate for the family as we sat around the fireside.

"We must do the presents," said my mother, smiling at little Henry who did not know what all the fuss was about. The drapes were tied back, and the early sun shone into the room melting the snowflakes that had settled on the windows turning them into little gems.

The presents were placed upon a table into separate neat piles, and we waited patiently for Henry to open his and we were all delighted to see the joy on his face as he discovered building blocks, and balls, and a rocking horse and his excitement grew with each new discovery as did the heap of ripped papers and ribbons. My parents appreciated the gifts we had bought for them; a new watch for Father engraved with heartfelt words of gratitude and love, and for Mother, a fur-lined evening cape because I had noticed how her regular one was beginning to fray at the hem.

I sat by little Henry as he played with a toy engine as Claude untied the first of his own gifts; it was a box that contained a fine silken hat and he placed it upon his head and smiled at my parents who had bought it for him.

"It fits with perfection; I knew it would. There is another to go with it," my father said, as he pointed to a larger bundle tied with an elaborate bow.

Claude unwrapped an exceptional coat of plum velvet adorned with gold buttons. His face lifted when he saw how fine it was and he slipped it on and twirled to show all of us how splendid he looked. His new outfit was instantly familiar and my whole body felt cold even as I sat by the burning fire. A suspension crept over me as I waited for my thoughts that were stumbling around inside my head to catch up with the dread of the realisation that was slowly building. The bottom seemed to fall out of my stomach as Claude unwrapped another parcel that had his name fastened to it and out of that packet, he pulled a doll.

His smile fell as he fingered the toy, its fractured pale porcelain face caught the sunlight and the whole thing shone in his hands like a vast jewel before he dropped it and reached out for me, calling my name from his own blanched face. His voice was now hollow and thin as though projecting from a place faraway. We all watched in horror as darkness appeared to envelop him, draining the colour from his plum coat. His sapphire eyes, once as blue as a cloudless summer sky, now became dark with blood-red pupils. I screamed his name and ran to take his outstretched hand but as I reached the spot upon which he stood he was no longer present; it was as though he simply blinked away.

During the aftermath, there was a silence so absolute, so terrible. Little Henry cried and was comforted by my mother as my father and I relentlessly searched for Claude. The doll lay broken on the floor where he once stood, and I saw the wrapping and recognised it as the same featureless brown paper trussed by ivy that I had once untied back at Star Lake. We searched until daylight receded and the house became steeped in the flush of a winter sunset. My father never gave up, he carried a lantern and combed the grounds till daybreak and whenever I looked into his eyes, I could see that during this darkest of hours, his scepticism of the old tales of Star Lake Hall had vanished like a mist.

I alone knew that searching at Holly Lane House was hopeless as I now understood the true horror of it. The man at the window had always been Claude, not Laurence as I had once thought. All this time I had seen a vision of the future, projected to me through the illimitable time of the *Christmas Room* itself. My mind was cast back to words Henry had uttered when lying broken in his bed, when he spoke of *her*, of Esther. He said she told him she would take his family, one by one. The spirit already had a room full of lost souls, but it seemed her strong desire for revenge is insatiate and she wanted more, *needed more*. I knew the only place where I could see Claude again.

During the days that followed I had fallen into so deep a dejection that if the sun shone, I did not see it, if the birds sang, I no longer heard them. My parents tried to console me, but I know not how to appraise my bereavement. Little Henry of course is a big comfort and a great worry. My days are now filled with anxiety, and I find I am an overprotective parent watching over him, never happy for him to be out of my sight even for a fleeting moment because I fear that like Claude, he could be snatched away from me. I tell myself that I saw no child in that room, but this fact alone is not enough to calm my worries.

I pray each day for Claude to be released back to me, oh, can my prayers avail me nothing? To feel the grief and to live with the heartache of all my hollow memories. Can I ever find peace in this hushed cry of sorrow? I feel crushed when I think of how Claude must feel, to be trapped in eternity, to gaze out of a solitary window able only to look upon his past. The room for him holds no sunlight, no warmth, no laughter, no music. Here he must remain confined in the darkness amongst the shadows of former lives, peering out from a window watching he and I as we were without means to restore the broken bonds between the living and the dead.

***

Eventually over time I plucked up enough courage to visit the ruins of Star Lake Hall and I stood with little Henry before the once grand doorway now open to the wind and the fauna. We stepped inside to complete our reconnoitre and accompanying us through the charred doors came a cool and silent wind that blew the fine powder snow that had settled upon the icy steps, and I thought back to all those dreams that had ushered me my whole life towards this very day.

Hand in hand we stood inside the shell of that once splendid house, in what had been the great hall. The upper floors were now burned away and exposed the firmament above, a steel grey sheet shadowed by cloud. I thought how the stars, those tiny pin pricks through the fabric of heaven would now shine down into this hollow space. For many months I had searched for our adjoined stars with a pathos that rent my heart. I could never see them again as much as I hunted; it was as though in the heavens as on earth I was now bereft of his light.

As the snow filled the spaces inside the house, shadows appeared around the ruins, and many were cast by tangled knots of creeper and by the remnants of wall and timber joists and some were not. There were moments under that leaden sky when shafts of sunlight pierced holes through the grey coverlet of cloud and the flickers of shadows appeared in the forms of people, some sitting, some dancing, and one who stood timeless, his back to the rest.

The author would appreciate an Amazon
and Goodreads review.

I do read all the reviews each and every one and
I am very grateful to anyone who has taken the
time to post a review. I appreciate the time you
have taken reading this book. I hope you enjoyed
reading it as much as I enjoyed writing it.

You are welcome to join David on his
Facebook page and group where you can
receive news about forthcoming releases, and
to discuss and share thoughts and queries
about any of David's published works.

https://www.facebook.com/davidralphwilliams

For more information on the complete
range of David Ralph Williams' fiction
visit David's website:

http://davidralphwilliams.simplesite.com/

Have you also read:

Sacred – Ghostly Tales.

Three traditional Victorian ghost stories.

For many, the ghost stories of old and particularly, from our Victorian forebears have always been popular. The Victorians excelled at telling them as they had an uncanny flair for capturing the feeling of malevolence and unearthly horror. Christmas eve has traditionally been the time to tell such frightening and eerie stories whilst seated around the fireside. Montague Rhodes James a principal of King's College Cambridge was a master of this art and would invite students and friends to his chambers each Christmas eve to listen in whilst he read to them one of his much-celebrated ghost stories.

I have been fortunate myself to have dined within the walls of King's College near the time of Christmas and have tried to absorb what residual atmosphere remains from these times of old. Thus, as in the great man's tradition I invite you to curl yourself around my hearth (metaphorically speaking) and allow me to tell you a ghost story, or three as it happens from within the pages of this book.

Don't be perturbed by tales of old country houses where malicious spirits linger and may, as one art curator discovers, become attached especially after removing something that is sacred to them.

Try not to dismiss the folklore of devils and other unclean spirits while working alone in solitude like my artisan of stained-glass attempts to do while trying to piece together the fragments of a broken window that once adorned an old sacred tower.

And under no circumstances ignore warnings of curses that surround infamous lost treasures as some things have remained lost for very good reasons.

Remain calm and take deep breaths because these new ghosts of Christmases past are gathering and are ready for you to discover them.

The following passage is taken from Sacred – Ghostly Tales:

As I unhooked the painting from its nail, I heard a sound from behind me, a gentle rumpling. Holding the portrait, I turned and saw a looking glass on the wall opposite. The glass had been covered by a mourning cloth, and the wrap had partially slipped down. I carried the painting over to the looking glass and I removed the mourning cloth and used it to wrap up the picture; the cloth would suffice as a protective cover against the elements outside as I carried it back to the station. One of the windows in the room had the remnants of a set of heavy, velvet drapes. There was a pull-cord dangling and frayed and I ripped it down and used it to fasten the cloth around the painting more securely.

Happy with my handiwork, I turned to leave the room but stopped firm in my stride when a casual glance again towards the looking glass revealed something indiscernible, shifting, and constantly redeploying itself upon the reflective surface. I rubbed at my eyes and tried to focus on the anomaly, now coalescing into – a form. I turned around to examine the wall behind but the figure in the glass was not a reflection of something in the room, it was it seemed, inhabiting the glass itself. I stood rigid with fright as slowly, and nimbly the figure climbed out from the looking glass, its lengthy cadaverous frame dropping to the floor. It crouched momentarily squat and hunched, with its face turned away from me, and then it seemed to uncurl itself as it straightened. It wore the clothes of a gentleman, although now outdated, and the apparel was old, ragged, and fusty. This impossible spectacle was akin to something experienced, I imagined, when under the effect of opioids. Finally, it turned and regarded me where I stood, paralysed by my fear.

It had a wrinkled, thin corpse-like face, pinched and trailing down to a tapered chin. Its mouth was a mere pinhole and yet it dripped a rancid slime as it sucked and blew out air as it sought to breathe. The thing had an unruly mop of black hair and it appeared to float about the head as though I was observing it underwater. It was a ghastly sight and I recoiled in horror of it. It looked at me full in the face. It was a terrible gaze. I must confess that I quailed under it, for it was a malevolent stare, full of hatred. With uplifted twitching hands, it advanced towards me.

David Ralph Williams has been writing
traditional ghost stories for many years.
David has written five previous books of ghost
stories and is co-author of the Paranatural
Detective Agency adventures. His latest work,
The Christmas Room and his previous work
Sacred – Ghostly Tales, are inspired by his love
of traditional ghost stories, particularly by the
works of MR James and Susan Hill and the BBC's
tradition of televised ghost stories for Christmas.
David currently lives in Cheshire in the UK.

Printed in Great Britain
by Amazon

UNSHAKEABLE WILL

YAHYE SIYAD

ISBN: 978-1-922956-06-4 (paperback)
          978-1-922956-07-1 (eBook)

 A catalogue record for this
book is available from the
NATIONAL
LIBRARY   National Library of Australia
OF AUSTRALIA

Printed in Australia by Ocean Reeve Publishing
www.oceanreevepublishing.com
Published by Yahye Siyad and Ocean Reeve Publishing

Ocean
REEVE
PUBLISHING